A Chemist

and

A Companion

Adriana Adams

WENDY MAY ANDREWS

Ellis Dorval

Sparrow Ink
www.sparrowink.com

ISBN - 978-1-989634-88-2

www.wendymayandrews.com

Stay in touch with Wendy May Andrews
and all her upcoming publishing news.

Sign up for her biweekly newsletter

Contents

When handsome scientists and High Society collide, chemistry is sure to follow...

Miss Adriana Adams is about to lose her position as paid companion. Fear for the future of her dependent family makes it hard to concentrate on finding a new position while still attending to her current duties. Meeting the handsome chemist inventing the most divine perfumes is only adding to her difficulties.

Viscount Severn relies on his chemistry compounds for both spending money and distraction. His uncle's efforts to disinherit him by siring a son has only resulted in strained relations, seven sweet female cousins, and two dead aunts. What Ellis doesn't need is the distraction of yet another female, even if this one is a lovely but timid woman nearly as fascinated by his science as he is.

Focusing on intellectual pursuits will keep their hearts safe, but what of the youngsters who depend upon them? How can they discover that a dry future really isn't the best choice?

If you love the wit and regency of Bridgerton but the wholesomeness of The Hallmark Channel, read Wendy May Andrews' latest Sweet Regency Romance Adventure.

Dedication

In *A Chemist and A Companion*, Adriana and Ellis are both looking for families of their own to call home. We all need that and I truly wish that for you. I hope you are safe and warm with a family of your own while you enjoy this great read

XO

Acknowledgements

Acknowledgment number one has to go to my truest companion, Mr. Andrews. Thank you for knowing and caring about my Gentlemen nearly as much as I do. My writer's journey has been an adventurous ride. It was much improved by being on it with you. You're the best partner a lady could ask for. Thanks for everything – totally vague but all encompassing.

Acknowledgment number two must go to my parents. Thank you for always supporting me in my endeavors. I love that you have read all of my books, even multiple times. Thanks too for reading to me when I was little – you started me on the road of a love of words.

To my beta readers – Alfred, Monique, Suzanne, and Christina – thank you so much for cheering for my characters, finding the plot holes, and making great suggestions to make my stories better.

My gorgeous cover is thanks to the artistry of Andrew at Sparrow Ink.

Thanks to Bev Kaufman and Julie Sherwood for the great edits. Any remaining mistakes are entirely the author's fault.

Chapter One

W*ell, that was interesting.* At least far more interesting than her usual existence. It was unlike her to put herself out there like that, making herself visible. Why would she offer to help the noblewoman? They had never even been introduced. But everyone, even the lowly companion, Miss Adriana Adams, knew who Lady Evangeline was.

These thoughts chased each other unhelpfully through Adriana's mind as she hurried away from the beautiful lady's side. Even though it had been out of character for her to have put herself forward like that, she hadn't been able to stand by when the lovely Lady Evangeline had been accosted by a strange woman. Despite the lady's fame, though, no one else had stepped forward to help her.

"You ungrateful wretch!"

The words hadn't been overloud, but there had been a sort of lull in the cacophony of the event as sometimes occurred in a crowd, and all heads had turned in their direction.

It was the whispers, though, that had made her do it.

It had seemed instinctive for Adriana to step up beside Lady Evangeline and stare down the obviously deluded woman. Adriana's instincts had rarely steered her wrong before, but it was most unusual for them to lead her to making herself so very noticeable.

"Contain yourself, Sabina," Lady Evangeline had all but hissed while keeping a pleasant smile upon her tight features.

"Why should I?" the strange woman had countered, still louder than was warranted, but she had lowered her volume and her belligerence slightly. Dria complimented herself that it was her own presence that had caused the adjustment, but it could have just been the other woman's shame catching up with her. Sabina, or so Lady Evangeline had called her, kept darting her gaze between the noblewoman and the unknown standing at her side. Perhaps she had been counting on Lady Evangeline's isolation. Adriana couldn't regret her impulsive move.

But the moment had passed, and now it was time for her to get on with her own affairs.

Affairs wasn't exactly the right word. That sounded far more interesting than what her life involved. But she needed to return to it, regardless.

Even when it had turned out Sabina was Lady Evangeline's disgruntled sister-in-law, Adriana couldn't regret taking a stand beside the noblewoman, protecting her from the whispers that would have circulated through the ballroom over a salacious scene. But she wasn't about to prolong the moment. She hurried back to the safety of the sidelines as soon as Lady Evangeline's friends arrived to flutter around her. The woman had barely acknowledged Dria's presence before she was gone. But that was totally fine by Adriana.

The life of a paid companion, it could be argued, not that she ever would argue, quite required invisibility and anonymity, at least in her experience thus far. Despite not even reaching the first quarter century of her existence, Miss Adriana Adams had already been a companion for more than fifteen years. So, she could confidently say she had experience.

In an effort to be reasonable, though, Adriana had to acknowledge that her experience, while extensive, was not varied. She had only been companion to two different people. As a child, she had been hired to accompany Miss Mary Lockwood. Mary was a poor orphan. Well, not poor in the financial sense of course. She had been extraordinarily wealthy from what Dria came to later understand. But she had been poor in the sense of sad, lonely, and really quite spoiled.

Adriana's family had been paid quite well to send her to live with Mary. They took their lessons together, played together, fought like sisters, and lived their lives together every day until Mary's guardians decided she needed someone with more sophistication to teach her how to go on as she debuted. That had broken both girls' hearts. Adriana had resolved never to grow attached after that. She hadn't quite realized up until that point that she wasn't *actually* a companion. She was a *paid* companion. That one small word altered the entire scenario.

Thankfully, Mary's guardians weren't completely heartless. They realized the Adams family had grown quite accustomed to the income Adriana generated, so they found her another position, accompanying Miss Bastion, a wealthy, independent young woman who required company to remain respectable as she traveled and explored and did all sorts of less than perfectly genteel things. But she was well to do and, with Adriana by her side, had a very proper companion, so she was considered acceptable.

So acceptable that she was about to wed, and well, with Viscount Droitmuir.

Adriana was happy for Miss Bastion, of course. Miss Bastion was over the moon with her fiancé and could hardly stand the wait before they wed. But she was also determined to have a grand, "important" wedding so wait she must.

It was a relief for Adriana that the woman wanted such a grand affair for her nuptials as it gave her a little time to figure out what she ought to do next. Her family wasn't going to accept her back without employment despite the fact that she had been supporting them for so long, or perhaps because she had done so. She hadn't seen her family in over ten years. All she knew of them was from letters. But those letters arrived weekly, reliably. And they kept her in line.

Whenever she considered finding some sort of employment where she was less dependent on the whims of another, a letter from home reminded her that wasn't an option for her.

Just this week, her mother had written: *"I know you are troubled about what to do next, but we are relying on you to figure it out, dear. We know you will not let us down."* Just thinking about that last sentence sent a clutch to Adriana's midsection. It was to be hoped her little stunt of supporting Lady Evangeline wasn't going to put a crimp in her employment efforts.

It was good that Miss Bastion's intended wasn't as eager as he professed, at least for Adriana. From what Adriana had seen of the *ton*, gentlemen could wed within days, hours even, if they were sufficiently connected and appropriately motivated. And if they weren't thusly connected, there was always the anvil in Gretna. But that was not for Miss Bastion and his stuffy lordship.

Adriana's eyes scanned the crowd. She ought to be in Miss Bastion's company. It wouldn't do to allow her to besmirch herself this close to reaching her final goal.

Not that the very proper woman would ever do anything improper. But she was very determined about appearances. It was surprising she had allowed Adriana even a moment of independence that evening. And how had Adriana used it? Did she dance or meet others or even fetch herself a glass of punch? No, she made herself companion to another lady in need.

There might be something wrong with her, Adriana surmised. It was a compulsion. The need to be needed. She supposed, if she were to analyze the matter, it was likely quite understandable considering the circuitous nature of her thoughts and feelings. Her family needed her to be needed by someone. And Adriana wanted her family to feel something toward her, even if it was merely avarice.

It would be quite lovely if it were something other than avarice, to be sure. Something like caring or love or even friendship. But she had learned young not to count on such things. Avarice was actually far more dependable. As far as she knew, it wasn't something that ever went away. She could trust that her family would always want her income.

But that meant she needed a new source of said income. While that interesting woman, Lady Evangeline, might need her services, Adriana suspected it wouldn't be for very long with the way she and the mathematician were gazing at one another. And it wasn't likely, even though rumour said they would have the means to do so, they would be waiting for a grand wedding to display their wealth in a rather bourgeois fashion.

That was the rub. Miss Bastion was unwilling to listen to Adriana's thoughts on how High Society did not make showy displays of their wealth. Miss Bastion could not accept that it wasn't genteel to be flaunting her love and her money all at once.

And therefore, Miss Bastion was suddenly far less eager to help Adriana find new employment. Adriana couldn't decide if she even wanted a new position. Oh, of course, she needed one. There was no arguing that fact. After fifteen years of relying on her income, the Adams family wasn't about to happily allow her to take a break from earning. Adriana didn't even know what she would do if she were ever afforded the opportunity. What did people do who weren't in service? Well, in her case, there wasn't a great deal of difference between what she did in a day as compared to a woman of the *ton* except that the woman of the *ton* would be the one choosing what she did. Adriana participated in all the same sorts of activities but she hadn't chosen them. That was the difference. And that was the allure of finding a different sort of employment.

Of course, anything she knew how to do would either require being at someone else's beck and call at all times exactly as she was now, or would pay considerably less and would therefore be unacceptable to her family.

Even positions as companion came with varying wages. Adriana had been most fortunate in her two positions, really. They had been pleasant enough. And the wage had been generous. But now they were all dependent upon it, making it impossible for Adriana to pursue any other interests.

Such as: wouldn't it be lovely to be a clerk in a bookshop? Or to serve the sweets at Gunters? Or even join an accounting firm? Not that they were likely to hire a female for any of those positions, but they all seemed like they would be far more enjoyable than being always, every minute of every day, subject to the whims of another person.

And now she had to find a new person for whose whims she would subject herself.

Was it possible the lovely and pleasant Lady Evangeline and her mathematician beau might need someone to help with the accounting? Adriana really knew nothing about them, but the rumours were abundant. The gossips whispered that Lady Evangeline had a great deal of wealth that needed to be monitored. That could possibly serve as a new role for Adriana. And would fit in with her imagined interest.

If not, how was she supposed to go about finding a new person to accompany? She had never had to do the finding before. Mary's guardians had found her in the first place and then had found Miss Bastion to hire her after that.

Could she track down those guardians and ask them for assistance in this instance? Or perhaps Mary herself could help her. They had lost touch in recent years while Adriana was travelling with Miss Bastion and Mary had made her debut. Now she was wed and well ensconced on her husband's estate raising children. This year Mary hadn't even accompanied her husband for the Season as she was increasing again and unwell with it. But she had always been a reasonably good correspondent. Adriana would write to her. It was her most promising idea. She should have done it the moment Miss Bastion had accepted Viscount Droitmuir's proposal.

Mary had never truly forgiven her for leaving even though she had finally come to understand it wasn't Adriana's fault. She, like Adriana, hadn't properly understood that Adriana's parents were being paid for Adriana to stay with Mary. That had been a lowering thought for both girls. And when they were separated, it had been a great blow to the poor little orphan girl. It had been a blow to the girl who wasn't an orphan, too, but in quite a different way.

Adriana had been devastated to learn her family didn't want her to return to them. She was grateful for Miss Bastion's forbearance in the early days of their acquaintance. It had been very easy to make Adriana weep. But not anymore. Thankfully, that dire period hadn't lasted more than a couple of weeks. The melancholy had lasted longer, but Adriana had learned to hide it much better as time passed. She had been most fortunate that Miss Bastion hadn't turned her off right from the beginning.

Now she barely gave a passing thought to the fact that her family saw her as little more than a means of support. In fact, they thought she ought to be grateful for the opportunities she'd had. They weren't wrong in that regard. And Adriana was grateful. It had been delightful to go to school with Mary and learn all the things a young lady ought to know. And travelling with Miss Bastion had been an education in itself. One she didn't regret. But having a family and not being with them was a source of pain that was difficult to describe. It made her feel unlovable when she needed as much confidence as she could muster.

Thus, it was quite unlike her to have approached Lady Evangeline and stood by her side to offer her countenance after that strange woman had accosted her.

"Oh, Miss Adams, Lady Evangeline wishes to speak with you before you leave the ball this evening," a footman stopped her to say just after she had rejoined her employer.

Nerves clenched her jaw and midsection but she managed to smile and nod politely.

"What is that about?" Miss Bastion asked with a frown. "I am nearly ready to leave and I'm too tired to wait upon you and your whims."

Adriana nearly stamped her foot in frustration. Miss Bastion never had to wait upon her, it was always, always the other way around. But Adriana needed to remain in her good graces a while longer, at least long enough to get her recommendation. She swallowed her sigh along with her disappointment.

"I'm sure it is nothing of import. We needn't wait if you are ready to depart."

"Don't be daft, Adriana, we cannot stand up her ladyship. She is connected with the Northcotts and Viscount Simmons now, it would seem, let alone her own family's connections – her brother's an earl, don't you know? It wouldn't do to put her nose out of joint."

The hysterical laughter that threatened to overtake her was only kept in check by Adriana's clenched teeth. After a deep breath she felt in sufficient control to be able to redirect the conversation.

"Have you any idea how we might find the lady to see what she might want of me?"

"You should have asked that servant while you had the chance," Miss Bastion said with a tone of censure. "How should I know where the woman is?"

Thankfully Lord Philips' timing was impeccable. His approach was welcome for the first time in an age. Adriana could almost muster a smile for him.

"I know you are fatigued, my dear, but since you are still here, would you care to go a round on the dance floor with me?"

Miss Bastion preened but turned to Adriana with a commanding tone. "You now have about ten minutes to find the lady and see what she wants with you."

With a sinking heart, Adriana watched her employer flounce away on the arm of the rather plain viscount. Adriana wasn't certain what Miss Bastion saw in the gentleman other than an available and willing male. Her employer had never seemed the sort to be desperate to wed so Adriana couldn't say what had changed to make her so eager now. Lord Philips wasn't even that highborn and Adriana suspected he was more interested in the depths of Miss Bastion's bank accounts than anything else about her. But it wasn't for her to say. And now she had dithered more than was necessary. How was she to find Lady Evangeline in the crowded ballroom in ten minutes?

She was blessed to find the answer much sooner than expected. Since Lady Evangeline was somehow connected with their hostess this evening, it was possible most of the servants would be aware of her whereabouts. Adriana took a chance and asked the next servant she came upon.

"I was told Lady Evangeline wished to speak with me. Have you any idea where I might find her?"

Before the footman could respond, a deep voice from the other side of her shoulder spoke. "I can take you to her."

Adriana's years of enforced gentility prevented her from jumping or squeaking even though that was what instinct called upon her to do.

"Thank you," she murmured, even as she wondered if she had lost her mind for even considering following a stranger about the room. At least it was within the room. There was nothing salacious or scandalous about it. It was foolish of her to even think so. It was probably just the scare he had given her. And Miss Bastion's nasty humour playing havoc with her nerves.

"Have we been introduced?" the gentleman asked making Adriana want to frown. Wouldn't he know if they had been?

"I beg your pardon?" It was such a useful phrase, she thought with amusement even as she wondered if she was losing her mind for having such a wayward thought.

The handsome man laughed. "Well, yes, I know we haven't, but I meant to ask if you were going to stand on ceremony and remain mute until someone could perform the duty."

Adriana nearly burst into laughter even as she fought back the strange flutters that muddled up her midsection over the handsome man's attention being focused on her. “Oh, no, I am insignificant. You needn’t worry about ceremony of any sort with me.”

“Never say such a thing,” the gentleman scolded. “No human is insignificant, and certainly not such a lovely one as you.”

Adriana blinked in surprise. She was usually invisible. In fact, she went to great effort to be invisible. Miss Bastion didn’t take kindly to anyone noticing her overmuch.

Was he flirting with her?

The question that flitted through her mind stunned Adriana. She didn’t think it had ever happened in her entire, not so long life. But she had witnessed it while by Miss Bastion’s side, either the fortune hunters flirting with her or gentlemen of all sorts flirting with debutantes all over the place. It wasn’t terribly uncommon despite not being the most genteel of activities. Or rather, she had thought it ungenteel. But now she might rethink that opinion, as everything within her began to flutter in a not unpleasant manner. She couldn’t exactly call it pleasant. But it wasn’t unpleasant either. More like unexpected. Never having experienced flirting nor the flutters it produced, Adriana couldn’t decide if she liked it or not.

She certainly wouldn’t like Miss Bastion’s reaction if she were late to meet her, though, so she really couldn’t dally with this lovely gentleman.

And now the silence had stretched between them and she could see the man’s pleasant smile had stilled and he was suddenly stiffer than he had been while still watching her attentively. That was a feat considering they were walking through a crowd.

“How do you know Lady Evangeline?” the unnamed gentleman asked, reminding Adriana that she had likely been foolish. He hadn’t been flirting with her, he just wanted to know her name. She tried not to sigh as he continued with his questions. "She has only very recently left off her mourning and re-entered Society so she hasn't become very acquainted with too many."

Now Adriana arrived at the conclusion that he was suspicious. She nearly burst into hysterical laughter. Of course, her self-control wouldn't allow such ridiculous conduct either, but the temptation was there. There was absolutely nothing in the least suspicious about her. It was droll to even consider.

"I don't really know her. I was nearby when that strange woman, her sister-in-law as it turns out, accosted her earlier this evening and was in a position to offer assistance. She likely just wants to say thank you once more which is completely unnecessary but I thought it would be rude to leave without answering her summons. But now I'm putting you out and really, I should just return and wait for Miss Bastion."

The man stopped in his tracks. "You really must tell me your name. I am Ellis Dorval," he said with a bow. "Viscount Severn, to be exact, I suppose," he added as almost an afterthought.

Heat flooded her cheekbones and made sweaty prickles break out under her arms. She hoped her hand wasn't equally sweaty as he reached forward to shake it.

"And you are?" he asked.

"Miss Adriana Adams," she finally managed to stammer out. She wasn't usually this awkward. Not that she would really know since she wasn't usually the one being addressed. She didn't *think* she was this awkward but perhaps she had been misguided in her own opinion.

"I don't know about rude, but if her ladyship asked to see you, you can be sure she is eager to do so. It would be a disappointment to her to find out you had left without allowing her to do so. It is most likely she wishes to thank you again, as you suggested."

"Oh, thanks weren't necessary. I barely did anything, really. Anyone would have."

"Would they?" he asked with a lift to his eyebrows. "Did they?"

Adriana opened her mouth to argue but there was nothing to say. She didn't know how to argue and it would really do no good in any case. What was there to argue? No one else had stepped forward to offer any assistance despite the myriad staring gazes.

"Yes, well, how do you know her ladyship?" Adriana felt awkward as she turned the subject back upon him.

"We too have had the opportunity to assist the lady," he said with a wide smile. "Some of us fellows are students and one has been helping her with some mathematical issues that have come up for her."

Adriana frowned. Why would anyone need to enlist students to help with their maths? Of course, she knew the handsome gentleman who appeared to be courting the lady was a mathematician, she just hadn't realized he had brought students with him. Perhaps the lady hadn't been properly educated. It was kind of the gentlemen to assist her in that case. It had been drilled into Adriana by Mary's governess that proper ladies did not sigh. Adriana wasn't a titled lady, but she had always expected herself to be proper.

But the urge to sigh was likely caused by jealousy and that was also ugly and improper. The urge increased but was still within bounds to ignore.

Chapter Two

Ellis couldn't say why the young woman seemed so intriguing to him. She reminded him of one of his favorite gasses, perfectly useful on its own without the need for any other influences around it. Except this Miss Adams was a little affected. She was obviously well in control of herself, but he could see in the pulse at the base of her neck and the periodic widening of her eyes that she was much more affected than she wished to let on. Her hands never fluttered, her face remained calm, almost impassive, and even when her eyes widened slightly, they quickly returned to their usual steady watchfulness.

If only he could study her like he did his chemicals. Because she actually seemed more like one of them than even a gas or one of his favorite stars. One that didn't react immediately. Those ones intrigued him but were the most dangerous. Of course, studying a woman like that would likely cause a stir that he knew their hostess was trying to avoid. Or rather, their hostess *was* trying to cause a stir, just not the type his studying a woman so thoroughly would cause. The slight refinement was important, Ellis reminded himself with a small smile.

He was Viscount Severn. He had been raised from the cradle to go about in Society. He could do it with very little thought. But High Society was most definitely not where his heart was. He would far rather be in a classroom or a laboratorium.

Oh, he would fulfill his duty as viscount, if it came to it, which it very well might not. His uncle, the Earl of Beaverbrook, was giving it his best effort to ensure Ellis would not inherit. But thus far the poor man had only managed to sire seven daughters. At least those were the only ones who lived. Ellis had also lost two aunts in the process of the earl's efforts to gain a son. Those poor women had suffered pregnancy after pregnancy in their attempts to fulfill the earl's raving wish.

And his poor cousins. Ellis could hardly think of the girls without shaking his head. It must be a burden to know how unwanted they were. At least they had each other. Ellis only had one sibling, a younger brother. But Daniel was a source of irritation for Uncle Beaverbrook if nothing else. Uncle Beaverbrook frequently lamented the fact that his brother could sire two perfectly healthy sons while he couldn't manage a single one.

And that was why Ellis was so hated.

Well, hate was too strong a word, of course. The man tolerated him, coolly, for the most part. They visited quarterly for Ellis to remain updated on all things related to the earldom. While Beaverbrook was determined to supplant Ellis in the succession, he would never leave his estate unattended. So, he dutifully trained his nephew in all manner of things. Deadly dull things, unfortunately. But Ellis knew his duty and knew every single nook and cranny of the estate and holdings that would become his if his uncle were to leave this mortal coil without fathering a son.

And so here he was at a Society event perfectly versed in how to go on. And fascinated with the frigid woman at his side.

It would be all the more interesting to see what Evangeline wanted with the woman. Adriana Adams.

Even her name sounded like it could be a star. Well not the Adams part but Adriana was a beautiful name. Worthy of celestial beings. He ought to have studied astronomy rather than chemistry if he were going to wax poetic on the topic.

He forced his thoughts back to the matter at hand. It wouldn't do to wander out of the room in his mind. Not while on an important errand, at the very least. He could commune with his stars and chemicals later.

Drat. Not later. They were in Town. It was unlikely to be clear enough to see with all the smoke billowing from every building. He didn't sigh. That would be too common. But he wished to do so. Or kick over the ridiculous potted plant that suddenly appeared in their path.

"Have you been in Town very long?" he finally inquired, remembering he was trying to learn about the quiet woman trailing beside him.

"Since the beginning of the Season this year. Miss Bastion wished to experience the entire Season even though she made her debut years ago."

Ellis found the lack of information nearly as fascinating as what she said. Who was Miss Bastion and why would it matter to this lovely creature?

"I see," he said, even though he did not. He found such mysteries to be quite like the mouse his cat had cornered under the wardrobe. He would focus on it until he had it solved. Unless he called himself to account and managed not to be that ridiculous.

Finally, she surprised him by speaking up. "Did you say you are a student?" she asked in a quietly surprised tone.

"A bit long in the tooth for school, you think, eh?" he asked with a chuckle. "We have graduated long since, of course, but we are professional scholars, the lot of us. All different specialties, of course, but we cannot leave our studies behind even if we have left school. And some of us have done well enough that the schools invite us back from time to time to teach them a thing or two. It is a thing of beauty to have that happen, to be sure."

"I can only imagine," she said in a breathy tone that made Ellis feel inexplicably important, as if she were admiring him rather than thinking him ridiculous for 'playing at science' as his uncle always growled. Ellis' parents hadn't been much more enamored of his studies than the earl, but they had at least done their best to tolerate it or at least not say too many derogatory things about his catalysts and compounds.

Of course, that one little explosion had done little to enamor his mother with his experiments. But in his defence, he had been little more than ten years old when that had happened. One couldn't expect a child to be as precise as they ought to be at that age. After the fire, though, Ellis had never had another mishap again. And it had been nearly twenty years since that one mistake.

And it was all paying off. Or was about to, if he could just find a way to manage his work on a little larger scale. Roderick was certain he could make a go of it.

But thinking about business was for another time, not something to discuss with the beautiful creature who had just asked him something if the expectant expression upon her face was anything to go by.

"I beg your pardon, I didn't hear you over the sound of the orchestra," he said less than truthfully. He had been wool gathering was the actual fact, but he didn't think she wished to hear that.

"I asked what you are studying. I haven't known any scholars before," she added, and Ellis acknowledged that he hadn't imagined her admiration. He tried not to strut as he continued by her side. He could see Lady Evangeline just ahead so he wouldn't have the woman to himself for much longer.

"Chemistry is my specialty now, although I have studied many things through the years."

"Chemistry," she repeated. "Are you not nervous of the noxious nature of some of your experiments?"

"Not particularly," he answered immediately. "Have you had a bad experience with chemicals?"

"I've not had the opportunity to study in any great extent, but we did have a bit of an accident one time when I was a girl. It has given me a healthy respect for mixtures and tonics ever since."

"That is the exact correct reaction, in that case," he acknowledged readily. "If you respect the elements, you don't have too much to fear."

"But some things are truly dangerous, are they not?"

"Yes," Ellis had to admit. "But if you know what you're doing, there is nothing to be troubled about."

He could see that the woman's attention had landed on Evangeline and even though she had seemed to calm down as they walked and talked, he could see that the pulse of nerves had returned to her neck. If not for that slight detail, there would be little to reveal the woman was nervous. His curiosity was well and truly piqued, and he wished he could spend more time with her. But that wouldn't be seemly.

Beaverbrook had started lecturing Ellis about his need to wed and produce an heir, just in case, which was why he was present that evening. Procrastinating on the matter was Ellis' favorite pastime, but he was certain the earl wouldn't want him dallying with an innocent unknown woman no matter how lovely she seemed.

The earl expected his heir to wed an earl's daughter at the very least. Preferably the daughter of a marquis or even a duke. Which was silly considering the earl was trying to disinherit him. What duke of the realm would wish to marry their daughter to a lowly Mr. Dorval if he were to lose the title of Viscount Severn to a young male cousin should his uncle succeed in producing a son?

Ellis was dithering again. It wasn't like him. A chemist needed to be precise and careful or else he would run into the sorts of trouble Miss Adams had been concerned about. But for reasons he couldn't fathom, he didn't wish to deliver the lovely young woman to his friends.

That was the rub, he realized with disgust. Evangeline was surrounded by a group of the scholars. Ellis didn't want to share Miss Adriana Adams with the other scholars for fear one of them would be as fascinated with her and succeed in making off with her. Not that any of the fellows would do anything nefarious with a genteel woman. But they might find themselves married if they weren't careful. They were dabbling in Society after all.

Suppressing the urge to shake his head, Ellis turned to the woman and gestured toward Evangeline. "We have found our quarry," he said with a smile.

"We were turned into hunters?" she asked with a smile. Ellis always appreciated it when others caught his humour even when it was a small attempt.

"One could argue a ballroom is nothing more than a hunting ground," Ellis pointed out in a low voice as they neared his friends, but he could hear Miss Adams' puff of laughter despite how stifled it was. He wished he could turn and gaze at her once more or even go so far as to give her a rakish wink. But he wasn't the rakish sort and winking was likely to gain him a lecture from Lucy so he didn't even turn to look at her. She wasn't his responsibility, no matter how much he was plagued with the urge to do her a service of some sort. He sensed she was in need of something, but he couldn't fathom why. He was not usually the empathetic sort.

That was one of the other scholars, Torrance's area of study. The psyche. It was rather fascinating stuff if one could get past the sensation that it was all hocus pocus.

No, Ellis preferred facts, elements, maths, reliable substances. Perhaps because so much of his life was out of his control. Like his entire future. It was dreadful that the security of his future was dependent upon his uncle dying before siring a son. *What sort of world was it that was arranged in such a way?*

It was far better for him to find his own source of security. And for that he relied on his science. And the friends gathered before him.

"I believe I have found someone you were searching for?" Ellis said to Evangeline with a slight bow before stepping back and presenting Miss Adams. After that he made himself scarce. Lovely young women of the *ton* were not for him.

Well, they were, but not until he had settled his own future. If he were to remain Viscount Severn or become the Earl of Beaverbrook, he would of course require a woman of the *ton* to partner with. For now, with the potential of becoming mere Mr. Dorval, he needed to remain focused on his goals.

No distractions allowed.

Chapter Three

Adriana wished for a brief, wild moment that she could remain hidden behind the gentleman's broad back. But one does not hide behind gentlemen, not even handsome viscounts who appeared as charming as anyone Adriana had ever encountered.

Obviously, he was not for her. Dalliances had never been for her but all the less so now when she was so desperately in need of procuring proper employment for herself.

"Miss Adams, thank you for coming to see me. I would have sought you out myself but, as I'm sure you can imagine, my evening has been a bit out of my control."

"Not at all, my lady," Adriana answered nonsensically, but really what else was she to say? She didn't know what the woman wanted of her nor did she properly understand what was going on with the lady and her circumstances.

"It has been brought to my attention that you might be in need of a new position," Lady Evangeline said in a gentle tone, watchful of her reaction.

Adriana opened her mouth to reply but wasn't sure what to even say to that. She merely shut her mouth and nodded. It was true, although she couldn't fathom why the other woman would care.

"I might have need of your services, at least for a time," Evangeline continued, making the light dawn upon her. A mixture of relief and disappointment filled her. For so many reasons she couldn't dwell upon at the moment, Evangeline's words were disappointing. Before she could object, the noblewoman explained a little further.

"I haven't fully examined the matter, but I think a paid companion could help me remain perfectly proper as I finalize my takeover of my late husband's business affairs." She lowered her voice and added, "And you could also act as chaperone as I pursue a courtship."

It was not an offer of friendship. It was a temporary offer at best. And it was a rather public one so therefore embarrassing and less than appropriate circumstance to be discussing such affairs.

"Thank you for your consideration, my lady, but I'm afraid a temporary arrangement might not be the best choice for me. For one thing, I cannot say that I have immediate availability as I must attend Miss Bastion until she is through with me."

To Adriana's surprise, her words seemed to please the lady. She smiled and nodded before continuing. "Perhaps both of you could consider attending me, in that case. You could assist us both and Miss Bastion would be freer to make her arrangements."

Adriana was shocked by the extent of the lady's knowledge, but here and now was not the time to discuss such matters. She had to return to Miss Bastion before that one took exception to her inattentiveness.

Lady Evangeline struck Adriana as being nearly omniscient when she nodded as though Adriana had spoken. "Perhaps you could prevail upon Miss Bastion to call upon me one day quite soon. For the time being I am in residence at Everleigh House, at least for another couple of days. We could more comfortably discuss the possibilities there."

Adriana's smile felt tight as she dipped a curtsy with a nod and barely another word, taking her leave and hurrying away to find Miss Bastion. She didn't even thank the pleasant viscount for his assistance. But what was there to say? Everything now felt at sixes and sevens.

She didn't imagine that anyone really enjoyed uncertainty but, ever since she had been informed she was no longer needed with Mary, Adriana had felt intense loathing for the sensation. It had upended her life. Which was odd. One could be excused for thinking her being taken from her home and brought to live with Mary would have been the incident that upended her life. But that had seemed like a delightful adventure. She had thought Mary was akin to a sister for her. A chum of her own age. They did everything together just as sisters ought. But when Mary's guardian came and explained everything more fully and clearly to her when she was seventeen years old, it had shattered the illusion of sisterhood and created uncertainty that she had never fully recovered from. It was truly foolish of Adriana that she had never realized her family was being paid for her to keep Mary company. She supposed it had never occurred to anyone to explain it to either of the two little girls. But it was an indisputable fact of her life that had left her in a state of uncertainty.

Now things were more uncertain than ever. What could Lady Evangeline want from her? Temporary? Of what good would temporary be for her? But of course, Miss Bastion would insist upon accepting. What a coup it would be for her. She would argue that it would also elevate Adriana's status, but it would only prolong the unstable nature of her life. She would need to find yet another employer after Lady Evangeline if that lady did in fact engage her services for a period of time.

Stop fretting. She admonished herself firmly. If she did remove to accompany Lady Evangeline for a time, that would give her more opportunity to contact Mary and her guardians, or rather former guardians now, she supposed since Mary was now a mature married lady. Adriana knew this was likely akin to hysteria. Or as close as someone who exercised as much control over herself as Adriana did could get to hysteria. Her thoughts were chasing themselves around in her mind like a dog trying to catch its tail. Not at all a productive state of affairs. And not one conducive to tolerating Miss Bastion's drawling narrative about her delightful evening on Lord Philips' arm.

"Now out with it, Dria, you've been sitting there like a cowering mouse under the broom for the entire ride home. What did Lady Evangeline want of you, and why didn't you remain with her to cultivate the relationship? Surely it would have done us both some good to be friendly in those quarters."

Adriana knew her chin had dropped, leaving her mouth agape like a fish, but she could barely contain her shock. Why would she now be saying she ought to have remained with Lady Evangeline? Miss Bastion had insisted Adriana return to her side by the end of the dance. It had been of average length. She hadn't quite managed it with chatting with the lovely viscount and her brief conversation with her ladyship, but Dria had done her best to ensure she hadn't kept Miss Bastion waiting a moment longer than necessary. But complaining of injustice had never done her any good in her life thus far; it wasn't likely to start to do so at this late juncture.

"If you are interested, we could continue the conversation another day, Miss Bastion. Lady Evangeline has invited the two of us to call upon her while she is in residence with the Northcotts at Everleigh House."

"What?" Miss Bastion nearly shrieked the question. "You beast, how could you have kept that information to yourself these twenty minutes or more?"

Adriana smiled. Miss Bastion really wasn't a terrible sort. She knew the other woman didn't mean her insults. And there was no way she was going to point out that she wouldn't have been able to tell her with her droning on about the ball.

"I do apologize, Miss Bastion," Adriana began.

"Oh, please, you needn't be quite so formal while it's just the two of us. We have been together for years now."

"Yes, of course," Adriana returned but still didn't say her employer's given name. It had been a contentious point for years. Miss Bastion nearly always wanted formality between them, and Adriana didn't really mind. It kept it straight in her own mind that this was an employer and underling situation, not one of friendship, and certainly not a familial relationship. She had no wish to make that mistake again.

"Well, hurry up, out with it, I'm near to perishing from the suspense," Miss Bastion urged, making Dria laugh a little, but she wasn't certain if it were true amusement or nerves.

"She was wondering if she might gain my, or our, services," Adriana finally blurted.

"Our services? But we don't have any services to render." Miss Bastion's frown was more puzzlement than irritation, Dria was relieved to note.

"She had somehow heard or ascertained that I will be in need of a position when you wed. She said she might be able to offer me a temporary one. But I pointed out that I wasn't quite available just yet, which she countered by saying that we might all three of us offer one another companionship and support during a time of transition. And she asked us to call upon her at Everleigh House at our earliest convenience."

Stunned silence followed Adriana's words, but that didn't last long. Miss Bastion's shriek was low but filled with delight as Dria was nearly certain would be the case.

"Everleigh House and the Northcotts. Oh, Dria, what a boon this will be for me. I knew you would remain loyal right to the end. Thank you, my dear. How marvelous this will be."

Adriana opened her mouth to object. She hadn't accepted. She didn't know if she wanted to do so. How was she to be companion to two very different women? It seemed to her that Miss Bastion would get all the benefits and all she was going to get was extra work. There hadn't even been any discussion of compensation or time commitment or anything that might be involved. Dria wasn't ready to commit herself without much more information.

But Miss Bastion wasn't thinking of any of that.

"We can let our lease go, which will give me more ready money to put toward the wedding," she was saying. "I shan't have to worry about you. But I'll be able to host some entertainments from Everleigh House. Oh, Dria, I'm going to be able to become a leader of Society just as I always knew I ought to be."

Disquiet clenched in Adriana's midsection. She ought to have warned Lady Evangeline about this eventuality. She should have declined outright and then thought of an alternate tale to tell Miss Bastion. This was worse than she could have even imagined. Dread began to mount within her as they pulled up in front of Miss Bastion's home. Or rather, their leased abode. Since they had been travelling nearly constantly since they had become acquainted, Miss Bastion had never seen the need to buy her own home. They had always rented rooms or stayed in hotels. It had been the most scandalous thing Adriana had ever been a part of, so that told a great deal about her, she thought with a grimace.

"We shall call round tomorrow at the earliest possible opportunity. It wouldn't do to arrive before the lady has left her chamber, but we wouldn't want to miss her either. Oh, Dria, how simply marvelous."

Adriana had never seen her employer quite this animated before, not even when she had become betrothed to Lord Philips. While she was certain they had not contracted a love match, it was disconcerting to witness the other lady being more delighted about a potential new friendship than her affianced husband. But that wasn't for Adriana to be troubled about, she assured herself.

What she was genuinely troubled about was what she could possibly say to interrupt this delight. Not that she wanted to quell the other woman's joy. Dria didn't begrudge her employer any of her good fortunes. She wasn't ready to commit to this venture without a great deal more information, but she was afraid she was going to be plowed into it by Miss Bastion's very eager determination.

"You really ought to be more excited, Dria," Miss Bastion pointed out. "This could be perfect for you."

Adriana managed not to snort in derision. How could it possibly be perfect for her? Having two employers sounded like a nightmare of epic proportions.

As though she might have heard her thoughts, Miss Bastion continued, "I know it might be a lot of work or perhaps confusing at times, and of course, we haven't even really heard what Lady Evangeline has to say, but moving in more exalted circles is going to open more opportunities for you."

"You mean to find another employer when this is all over?"

"No, silly, as I've told you often enough, you really ought to marry. It isn't as though there haven't been opportunities from time to time over the years. I've never understood why you have never accepted. It would surely provide you more security than being my or anyone else's companion."

Adriana didn't bother sighing. It was rude and wasn't genteel. Or at least that's what was drilled into her head by Mary's governess when they had been children. And Dria believed it to be true. But if ever there was a time for sighing, it was now. Miss Bastion might have told her over and over that she ought to wed, but Dria had countered over and over that she couldn't wed someone of a similar station to herself as that would leave her family without support. And the thought of marrying someone above her made her want to take to her bed with nervous fits. She couldn't bear the thought of the snickers and comments members of the *ton* would make toward her for reaching so above herself. No, Adriana Adams knew how to keep her place. She would never again suffer the experience she had as a girl, being told she wasn't important enough to be Mary's companion anymore.

Dria knew enough about the inner workings of the mind to realize that experience was colouring all others. And that in this case, once one was wed, it was a permanent arrangement. But there hadn't been any well-born gentleman interested in her anyway, so it was rather a moot point. And she couldn't marry someone without deep pockets. So that left her some bourgeois *cit* to wed or she remained in service. And why would one of those want to marry her? She couldn't elevate his status in any way, she was just barely gentry. In service she had control over her affairs to at least a certain extent. And she could remain around the fringes of the only world she'd really ever known. It was the closest thing to a sense of security she was apt to achieve in this life. And it was currently being threatened by this new development.

Or that's how it felt to Adriana at any rate. New exposures caused fear. That wasn't necessarily rational, Dria didn't suppose, but it was the situation she was facing. And face it she would.

If Miss Bastion insisted, she would do her best to accompany them both. She hadn't a clue how she could manage that. But surely Lord Philips would soon insist that a wedding date be set and the marriage could proceed, and then Adriana would be left with only one employer until such time as that fine lady decided she was no longer required.

And that was really the issue for Adriana. Prolonging the uncertainty was only going to drag out her personal turmoil and suffering. She hated uncertainty like it was a dread disease. She tried to avoid it at nearly any cost. But she had no desire to offend Miss Bastion at this juncture.

A sigh threatened but Adriana was once again able to swallow it down. She was far too genteel for such behaviour. In her tumult she was becoming tediously repetitious within the recesses of her mind, but there wasn't much she could do about it.

Miss Bastion laughed. "You are being a goose, Dria. You ought to be even more delighted by this opportunity than I am. Even if you wish to remain employed rather than truly settled, you will have more opportunities to meet potential employers moving around in the Northcotts' circles, don't you think?"

She did have a point, Dria acknowledged, feeling some of her flutters settling down. It was entirely possible she could be settled shortly. Perhaps Lady Evangeline could even realize she might need to retain her services.

Not likely considering her own betrothal had just been announced that night. From what she had observed of the decisive young woman, she was likely to have her marriage finalized before even Miss Bastion.

But there was no sense in fretting at this point. She would know more when they made their call. Possibly within hours. The thought should be comforting. And it was in a manner of speaking. At least some aspects of the uncertainty would be answered before she had too long to agonize over it.

But she would agonize anyway. She was good at it. Not that anyone could tell. At least not most of the time.

"Thank you for not saying no right away." Miss Bastion surprised Adriana as they climbed the stairs to their bedchambers.

"I beg your pardon?"

"I'm sure you would have preferred to tell Lady Evangeline no thank you as soon as she uttered her invitation. You could have just made up some tale with me and I might never be the wiser."

Dria found a smile from somewhere. "You know I'm not that creative."

Miss Bastion laughed. "Perhaps not terribly, but I'm sure you could have managed something believable. Thank you for not doing so."

Adriana was gratified by the rare display of warmth, and she bobbed a nod as they said their goodbyes in the hallway. What a peculiar night it had been.

Chapter Four

Lady Evangeline had invited that woman to join their motley group at Everleigh House? How very strange. Even stranger was Lucy's reaction. Ellis would have thought the woman would be disappointed to hostess still more company but somehow, she behaved as though Evangeline had done her a great service. She had even said so.

"How did you know I would wish to be involved with those two?" Lucy had gasped as though the lady had gifted her the greatest boon she had been wishing for. To Ellis' surprise Lady Evangeline, Sean, and Roderick had all laughed as though they understood the cryptic words. But none of them appeared inclined to explain their odd behavior.

Ellis suspected Lucy had a determination to play matchmaker. The other scholars had thought as much when Lady Evangeline had turned up at the Scholarly Society and Lucy had been so delighted. But was she intending to matchmake all of Society? He didn't have time to ask.

"Good night," those four called out to him, almost in unison, as he took his leave of them and climbed the stairs to the large room the men were sharing. The other, less occupied gentlemen had invited him to carry on after the ball to some clubs or a den of some sort, but Ellis had been up early working on his experiment and hoped to do so again in a few hours. He had no interest in chasing after the wild set. That might not make him High Society material, but he had always known that about himself even if he was styled Viscount Severn.

Perhaps that was why his uncle was so set upon disinheriting him. Beaverbrook knew he wasn't truly noble. Except Ellis couldn't perceive anything noble about drinking oneself into oblivion or gambling away one's spending money. Or worse.

Ellis horded what funds he had. If he didn't inherit, he needed to be able to provide for himself. And he truly hated the thought of being dependent upon his uncle's death. He was determined to find the final element missing in his extraction technique. He was absolutely certain he would be able to make a small fortune if he managed to figure it out. He had time. Even if his uncle found himself a new wife who bore a son, Ellis had managed to save up enough of his quarterly payments through time to keep himself fed and housed for many months, even without Roderick Northcott's generous sponsorship. In fact, he had managed to convince Roderick that he didn't require any sort of allowance from him. But Ellis did happily accept the room and board they generously offered him. In exchange for that, along with the friendship of the other scholars, Ellis would happily share a small percentage of his proceeds with Roderick's Scholarly Society. It was a fair exchange. Ellis wouldn't have survived school without the other fellows.

He had loved being a student. Learning had been like food for him. But that eagerness to learn had earned him mockery and abuse from some of their classmates. In hindsight, Ellis supposed he could understand it. The fellow who was studying psychology would probably say the mockers were overcompensating for their own feelings of inferiority, but it hadn't felt to young Ellis as though those cretins felt any degree of inferior to him.

He had been small, intelligent, and not cared for by the peer he was to succeed. It had been a recipe for disaster. But Roderick Northcott and his band of misfits had taken him in and given him a sense of belonging. Despite Ellis' ingrained sense of independence and determination not to owe anyone a single grout, he was intensely grateful for the sense of family the others provided him. To that day, he had to acknowledge, despite the fact that he hadn't wanted to go to the clubs with the others.

Why was Lucy so delighted about having those women invade their space? And it was going to start feeling like an invasion if they had to be fashionable all the time. They barely ever saw the earl, so they could usually ignore the fact that they were the guests of such a high member of Society. Never mind that Ellis himself might sit in the same position, for now he was a mere impoverished scholar who happened to carry a courtesy title of viscount. Roderick and Lucy were never high in the instep. Lucy was the daughter and sister of a viscount and could be very much a lady when the need arose but for the most part, she was lovely and approachable and essentially the younger sister and mother figure of their awkward scholar society.

With Lady Evangeline in residence, they had all taken her in as one of their own because she had a problem they were uniquely equipped to help her with, figuring out her financial mess and whether or not she was actually an heiress. And now there was the matter of the treasure. Sean had come across the mention of it in a document he found in the lady's papers. Evangeline didn't believe it could possibly be real and so had agreed that the scholars could pursue it however they wished.

Some of the scholars had decided it was the lost library of Alexandria and they were determined to find it. Evangeline regarded it as a lark and didn't much care, but Ellis supposed that stemmed from the fact that she was extraordinarily wealthy as well as entirely distracted with figuring out how to manage that wealth. Having the mathematician become her fiancé was likely to help her work it out. Perhaps she would become more engaged in the hunt once that settled. But for now, whatever the case, she was one of them. A member of their ragtag family.

That could not be said for the very serious Miss Adams and the woman she accompanied.

Miss Bastion. Ellis had been introduced to her on one of the rare occasions Uncle Beaverbrook had insisted he turn up to some Society function. She had struck Ellis as somewhat meanspirited and unpleasant. He did not envy the lovely Adriana for her role as the woman's paid companion. What a thankless job that must be. He wondered why she was in service. Curiosity about her niggled at the back of his mind and he considered what scent he would associate with her.

Lucy was a summer rose. Light and pleasant and universally appealing.

The scholars were mink. Not the soft fur, but the musky odor. It could be considered pleasant most of the time. But not during a certain season. It was perfect for the cantankerous scholars who were jovially amusing when the science was in their favour but could turn to feral beasts when they couldn't work out a problem.

He was the same, he supposed. And the worst thing was, when his experiments went wrong, he had to live with the consequences until the stink wore off. There had been times when Lucy had banished him to sleep in the stables except Roderick worried the animals would suffer. Thankfully, those troubles were happening less and less often. He was relieved to note that he had been more successful than ever lately. Now he just needed to complete his machine in order to be able to recreate the process on a larger scale. Then he would have all the blunt he would need. He would turn his attention to other chemical compounds and lend his assistance to some of the others. Especially Lincoln Welby, their botanist, and Charles' studies of compounds to solve diseases, surely, he could use Ellis' help. His extraction techniques would be of particular use to them.

Next to feeling secure, feeling useful was Ellis' primary aim in life. Sitting around waiting for a relative to die was particularly good at making a fellow feel useless. And being mocked for losing at all the sports because of having his head buried in a book as a boy hadn't helped him much either.

Now that he had finally grown into his height, he was able to show himself to a reasonable advantage in most games of sport, but he still much preferred dealing with books than people. It was only his long years of training that ensured he could behave like the nobleman he ought to be rather than stutter like the bookworm he really was.

Ellis sighed. It was no wonder Uncle Beaverbrook thought he was a changeling and wished for another heir. But his seven daughters weren't enough to satisfy the man. He continued to try for a male offspring.

Those poor girls. Ellis wished he could force their father to pay them attention. He tried to compensate for their poor treatment within the family by bringing them treats and trinkets whenever he was forced to meet with their father, but his strict budget didn't allow him to be too generous, especially not when there were seven of them.

They could all be his responsibility one day. Well, surely not all of them. Some of the girls must almost be old enough to make their debut, Ellis surmised as his thoughts turned to the companion once more. Perhaps Uncle Beaverbrook would need her assistance for the girls. Ellis doubted the man was thinking about his daughters as he searched for a new wife. It was far more likely he was only thinking about her ability to produce more offspring, but he ought to be considering a wife who could help him with the children he already had.

With a shake of his head, Ellis tried to dismiss the many concerns. None of it was his to worry about. Yes, those girls were his cousins and yes, he cared about their welfare. But knowing his uncle the way he did, the man wouldn't welcome his interference.

Or perhaps he would when one thought about how little consideration the man gave to the matter.

But it was certainly something he could do nothing about that night. He would far rather redo his formula for the extraction he was hoping to achieve as soon as they returned to the estate. It was too bad Roderick and Lucy wouldn't allow him to bring much of his equipment with him to Town. There was a room that would have been perfect for his use.

With a mischievous smile, Ellis wondered if anyone would notice if he started clipping leaves and blossoms from the conservatory.

And if he wasn't mistaken, Everleigh House actually had an orangery. It was quite decadent for a London house to have one, but he wasn't about to complain. Orange notes were exactly what he was looking for in the scent he was working on. He would be sure some samples accompanied him back to the estate when they left.

Ellis hoped that would be sooner rather than later but from Lucy's determination to help all these women, he was suspicious that his hopes were only wishes.

Chapter Five

The turmoil in Adriana's midsection hadn't allowed her to partake of much breakfast that morning and she was grateful for her nearly empty stomach when the flutter of nerves grew worse as they pulled up in front of the Earl of Everleigh's grand townhouse. The carriage gave a slight lurch as it came to a stand and an echoing reflex had Dria clenching her teeth to prevent the few contents of her midsection from spewing about.

Wouldn't that be the utmost indignity? And surely it would put the lie to any claims she might make to gentility. *Not that illness respected social boundaries,* Dria acknowledged with a note of hysteria tinging her thoughts that even she could recognize.

"This is so exciting, Dria," Miss Bastion cooed as she reached for the handle on the door before a footman could do it for her. Adriana shook her head. Fortunately, from what she could tell, their hostess wasn't so high in the instep that she would notice, but Adriana had been trying to curtail Miss Bastion's impulses for years. Clearly to no avail.

The footman did arrive as Miss Bastion was stepping down, and he stood by to assist before handing Adriana out of the carriage. With a slight smile of gratitude to the servant, Adriana turned her full attention on the large house.

It was a testament to the Northcott wealth that they had such a grand house in the heart of the fashionable part of London. But the house was remarkably inviting for all its size and grandeur. Some of the flutters subsided for her, at least briefly, and for that she was grateful. But then Miss Bastion was hurrying up the stairs, and Adriana could do nothing but accompany her and hope all would end up well despite her fears.

More servants greeted them politely and efficiently upon their arrival in the entrance hall. The butler had them escorted to a receiving room while he sent someone to see if Mrs. Northcott was receiving.

Miss Bastion started to object, but Adriana discreetly pinched her. When her employer turned an outraged face toward her, Dria could see the rebuke just waiting to leave her mouth, but she gave her head a slight shake followed by a very brief but fierce frown and Miss Bastion managed to contain herself until they were left in the salon to wait.

"Why would you pinch me like that?"

"You were going to do something you ought not," Adriana pointed out.

"Well, the butler was going to find the wrong person. We asked for Lady Evangeline."

Adriana took a deeper breath than was warranted for the conversation, but it helped her contain all the things she didn't want to say and the tone she shouldn't use.

"While we did ask for Lady Evangeline, we ought to have asked for Mrs. Northcott, as she is the hostess of this home, it would seem, at least for now."

"Right." Miss Bastion acknowledged Adriana's words with little inflection before a couple beats passed and then she blew out a breath of frustration. "Thank you, Miss Adams, I appreciate your interference in this instance."

Adriana's eyebrows lifted on her employer's terminology, but she didn't bother arguing. She had interfered, she supposed. It was for Miss Bastion's benefit. But that lady didn't seem to appreciate it entirely despite the thanks. Dria tried to think the other woman could possibly be nervous too. But considering how much she wanted to be there, it wasn't likely. But at least she acknowledged that Adriana had been in the right. She wasn't irritated with her.

Dria hated her insecurities. Given the circumstances, they were likely understandable. But she still hated them and wished she could be rid of them. What must it feel like to belong to this home, for example, she wondered as she looked around the lovely room with its high ceilings, large windows, and remarkably comfortable looking furniture. The light fabric made her nervous, though. She wouldn't want to be the one responsible for keeping it clean and presentable. Not that she had ever had responsibility for any furniture, so that was a ridiculous concern, but Adriana had a tendency to feel responsible for everything. She supposed it stemmed from Miss Bastion becoming grumpy and confrontational with her when things outside her control went wrong. That made her always on guard to make everything run smoothly, even the things that shouldn't be expected of her. It wasn't really the best state to be in, but it was what she had. At least for a time. And now they were here in this lovely room to consider whether or not she might take on even more responsibility.

What a ridiculous notion. She needed that like she needed a kick in the head.

But she couldn't deny Miss Bastion. Not when her own future or that of her family was at stake. Adriana pinned what she prayed was a gentle smile onto her face and waited to see what would come of their visit. Surely, she would know shortly.

There was a bustle of activity and Mrs. Northcott burst into the room with Lady Evangeline following in her wake. Adriana had to smile over that imagery. Mrs. Northcott wasn't an overlarge woman, but the energy she contained made it seem as though a force had entered the room and she was merely bearing the other woman along in the energy she created with it.

"How perfectly delightful that you have come to call," Mrs. Northcott said, almost clapping her hands like a small child in her glee. Her bright disposition was infectious and Adriana felt her own spirits lifting with the other woman's boisterous humor.

It might be exhausting, but it could be delightful to be in this presence for a bit, she thought, for the first time feeling a little less full of doom over the prospect.

"Good day," Miss Bastion finally greeted the woman while Adriana stood and dipped a curtsy.

"Oh, no, please no formal ceremonies. We are to be friends, are we not?" Mrs. Northcott called with a trill of laughter.

"Thank you for coming," Lady Evangeline broke into the conversation. "I didn't intend for you to feel obligated to come immediately. I hope my summons didn't inconvenience you."

She was looking at Adriana, but it was Miss Bastion who replied. "Not at all, not at all. We were delighted to come and learn what your words of last evening meant. We would be most happy to be of any possible service to you."

Adriana winced over Miss Bastion's effusive words. It wasn't quite the thing to be that eager. Even she knew that, and she didn't mix with High Society often. But it was one of the lessons their governess had insisted upon when she and Mary were small. Everything had to be in moderation, even their excitement. It had been a challenging lesson to learn, but learn it they did. Now for the briefest moment, Dria wondered if the governess would emerge to rap Miss Bastion's knuckles with her ruler.

The imagery of that thought caused a ripple of laughter to shimmer through her. She managed to prevent it from coming out of her throat by the exertion of her will, but it lightened her spirits even further despite the struggle not to embarrass herself.

"Of course," Lady Evangeline was saying to Miss Bastion even as she took a slight step back. The movement must have called Miss Bastion to her senses as she was much more moderate when she continued.

"That is to say, we didn't have anything planned for today, after the ball, and since neither Miss Adams nor I are ones for lazing about in bed, it was no hardship for us to attend you today."

Adriana nodded her agreement. Miss Bastion had reached the right note and the slightly awkward moment passed without further comment.

"Shall we sit and have some tea?" Mrs. Northcott invited with a gesture toward the settee.

Once they were all settled and sipping warm cups of tea, Mrs. Northcott filled the air with her chatter. It was mostly nonsensical. The usual gossip one could hear in every drawing room of the *ton*, especially the day after a ball such as they had attended the night before. Dria was surprised there had not yet been mention made of Lady Evangeline's betrothal nor of the reason why she and Miss Bastion were present. But since Mrs. Northcott was the hostess, it wasn't for Adriana to question her choice of conversational gambits. But her teeth were starting to sit on their edge, and her patience was running low.

"Thank you, Lucy, that was delightful," Lady Evangeline interrupted the flow of Mrs. Northcott's words. "I will never cease to be amazed at your conversational abilities. You could win wars and influence history if you had a mind to do so."

Dria wasn't sure what exactly Lady Evangeline meant by her words, but it took all she had to prevent the twitch of her lips from turning into a grin of amusement over them. To her surprise, Mrs. Northcott didn't take any offence over her friend's words, merely grinning as though she had been complimented to the highest degree.

Mrs. Northcott nodded toward Adriana and Miss Bastion but kept her attention on Lady Evangeline. "Would you prefer me to stay or leave?" she asked, indicating she understood Lady Evangeline had things to discuss with the other visitors.

"Oh, no, you must stay, we've come this far together," the lady said causing an uncharacteristic spark of curiosity to come to life within Adriana's mind or chest or wherever curiosity lived. It was an unfamiliar sensation. Well, perhaps unfamiliar wasn't the right word. Perhaps unwelcome was better. Adriana had been an intensely curious child. Even into late girlhood. But when she had begun accompanying Miss Bastion she had learned to curb, ignore, and stifle the urges curiosity provoked within her. They were far from helpful. A curious person would grow wholeheartedly bored of the life of a paid companion. Adriana didn't have that luxury. So, she couldn't be curious. It was as simple as that. That made this an entirely inconvenient time for those old urges to resurface. But oh, how she wished she could ask her ladyship what she meant by her words to Mrs. Northcott.

How rude that would be!

And Adriana would never be rude.

So, she sat as still as possible and waited for further developments. Adriana was surprised to see that Miss Bastion too was perched beside her as though watching a presentation of some sort. And that was what it was, Dria acknowledged. The entire tableau had been a play, she supposed. Mrs. Northcott had merely been chattering to pass the time, perhaps to allow her friend to collect her thoughts or for some other reason she couldn't fathom. Whatever it was, it would seem Lady Evangeline was now prepared to proceed.

"Again, I would like to thank the two of you for coming to see me. I know it would have probably been more appropriate for me to come to you but for reasons I shan't go into at the moment, it was better for me to remain here."

Adriana had to work at not frowning in confusion over this jumble of words that didn't all make sense. She waited for the woman to say more.

"I could use the services of a companion, I would say. And I know you, Miss Bastion, will be marrying soon. Have you, Miss Adams, found future employment?"

"Not as yet," Adriana replied.

"It is likely an imposition to ask this of you, but would you consider being *my* companion as well for a time?"

"How could that work?" Miss Bastion asked before Adriana could offer any response.

"If the two of you removed here until I am able to move into my own home, there would always be someone to lend you countenance were your gentleman to come calling or accompany you when you need to go out. It would mean Miss Adams would be particularly busy for a time, but I would compensate her handsomely for her efforts."

Dria could see that Miss Bastion was delighted at the prospect and was about to accept on her behalf, but Adriana spoke up before she could. There was a myriad of questions she needed answered before she wanted to commit to such a thing.

"What sort of accompanying do you think to require? And for how long?"

Lady Evangeline huffed a breath that sounded suspiciously like a sigh, nearly shocking Adriana to her toes. The woman struck her as the most elegant lady she had spent time with. She never would have expected a sigh from her lips.

"I suppose I ought to explain some of the details, but I would ask, especially if you do not accept my offer, that you do keep my confidences, at least for the next few weeks."

"Of course," Adriana responded. She would never betray a confidence. Even Miss Bastion was nodding eagerly.

"I will be taking over most of my late husband's business dealings." She stated it in a tone that was a mixture of pride, trepidation, and embarrassment – an odd combination to be sure. Adriana had the impression the lady was fearful of their judgment for the unusual act. But Dria could only admire her for trying. "There is a degree of opposition from my late husband's family, besides the possibility of scandal. For both these reasons, I would like to have someone of impeccable reputation at my side. And Lucy can't be always at my beck and call. She would be better suited to accompanying Miss Bastion if needed on social-type things. So, you see, you shan't be left abandoned."

This last Lady Evangeline directed toward Miss Bastion, as though this was of concern to everyone in the room. Adriana had a sudden urge to roll her eyes, another unusual impulse. She wondered if she ought to even associate with this woman if it was going to ruin all her hard-won controls.

How could this one interaction have such an effect upon her? That was surely impossible. It must be the uncertainty of her future dragging her down.

"How long do you think to require my services?" Adriana piped up again. It would be beneficial for her to know how long the uncertainty would last. It didn't appear as though she had a great deal of choice in the matter. Miss Bastion was clearly all for the situation. And if she was going to be paid twice for the same time period, Adriana ought to be a little more enthused on the topic. Perhaps then she would be in a position to take a holiday somewhere. Perhaps Bath would be lovely for the summer. Or she could go visit her family.

Her heart nearly stuttered at that thought. It wasn't likely they would welcome her. But if she arrived with additional funds it was possible they would do so. Or they would tolerate her anyway.

"I am not completely certain of all my plans at the moment. We will remove to my new house on Spring Street as soon as it is ready for us but will likely spend a fair bit of time here. Other Northcott family members would like to come to Town, you see."

"Spring Street is a lovely location," Miss Bastion spoke up, even though Dria was certain she would be disappointed to remove from Everleigh House. But the draw of even more of the wellborn family was likely of consolation. It confused Adriana as to why the woman would need her if there were going to be so many others about to attend her. She wondered if she ought to voice her concerns.

"You may speak your mind. Please do," Lady Evangeline said. "While I do hope you say yes, I want your consent to be well informed."

Dria hesitated, knowing Miss Bastion would not appreciate her dissent. "I am just a bit unsure as to what you need me for. If you have Mrs. Northcott and her sister-in-law, surely they are in a far better position to lend you countenance."

"They are lovely," Lady Evangeline agreed with a smile directed at her friend, but she remained serious and returned her attention to Adriana as though she appreciated and respected the question. "But they have their own lives to lead. Lives that are a little more leisure oriented or perhaps home oriented is a better concept to use. They will be in the perfect position to replace you at times with Miss Bastion. But if I could have you at my beck and call, I will feel much better about the things I need to do in the coming weeks. Things for which my maid in tow might just not be enough to maintain my propriety."

Adriana stared at the woman unsure what to say. Would her own propriety remain intact? Would this make her less employable after this time period was over? She mentioned mere weeks. But then Miss Bastion would likely wed in that time. Surely, she couldn't drag her engagement out much longer. Then Dria could focus on only one employer. And on the search for a new one.

"I will also ensure, if you wish it, that you are securely placed before we part ways in a professional capacity," Lady Evangeline added.

"See, Dria, it's the perfect thing. You'll be extra compensated, and then you'll have your new situation arranged. You should be in alt not dithering about it," Miss Bastion scolded.

"I disagree, Miss Bastion," Lady Evangeline interrupted. "I am actually relieved that she is asking intelligent questions. It tells me she isn't looking for social advancement but is actually concerned about performing her duties. She is likely concerned about being able to accompany you and me at the same time."

"But I and my sisters-in-law will make sure Miss Bastion is well taken care of, have no fear Miss Adams," Mrs. Northcott interjected.

Adriana appreciated the reassurance. It was her concern. But she could also feel Miss Bastion nearly vibrating beside her. She wasn't likely to countenance anything other than acceptance from Adriana on this topic. Dria didn't even have the luxury of thinking about it. The matter seemed to be urgent. Both matters, really. Miss Bastion really wanted this, and she was her primary concern until that woman wed. And Lady Evangeline seemed to genuinely wish for her company. Or her assistance or however one would call it.

And Dria's main goal in life was to be needed. So really there was nothing to think about. Except she had one final question.

"But why me, my lady?" she had to ask despite knowing it was likely to provoke Miss Bastion's ire. "You could surely hire a perfectly appropriate companion of your own that wouldn't come with an added complication of a pre-existing employer."

Rather than take offence, much to Adriana's relief, Lady Evangeline nodded and laughed lightly. "You raise another valid, intelligent question," she said with approval in her tone that thankfully seemed to quell the irritation Dria could feel vibrating off Miss Bastion at her side. "It only occurred to me last evening when you stepped in to assist me that a paid companion would be such an asset to my situation. And since you were the only one of my acquaintance, and obviously well suited to my circumstances, I thought to ask you. And since Lucy is also inclined toward including the both of you in her plans, it struck me as a perfect solution to several problems."

Adriana didn't feel like that really cleared anything up, rather it left her with even more questions, but there was nothing else for her to say but, "When can we start?"

Chapter Six

"Why are you hovering about out here, Severn?" Roderick Northcott asked him with laughter clearly evident in his voice.

Sean Smythe was just behind him and he too was clearly amused. "The chemist is unused to the house being full of the fairer species," the mathematician said with a chuckle.

"Well, don't just stand there, man, join them. Lucy told us at breakfast that if any of the gentlemen were present when there were callers that we were to join them to say hello." Roderick sounded a mixture of indulgent and impatient.

"I'm fairly certain 'tis one of her projects, though, so be warned," Sean added even as he made to enter the room.

"Projects?" Ellis asked, confused.

"Ignore Sean," Roderick implored. "My wife is just eager to be of assistance to anyone she encounters. It is one of her most endearing traits."

"She thinks she stole a march on the other ladies the Season she nabbed our Roddie here," Sean interjected with another one of his rather maniacal chuckles. "I suspect the visitors might be a part of that, just like my Evie."

Ellis wasn't sure if he ought to believe what Sean was saying and Roderick was only shaking his head with an indulgent smile so that didn't quite indicate whether it was true or not. In either case, they were all going into the withdrawing room, it would seem, as the butler and housekeeper approached with more refreshments.

Roderick pulled open the doors and entered with Sean and Ellis following close behind. "Are you finished discussing your private matters, ladies? Are we too early or too late to join you?"

Ellis didn't hear what was said as his attention was, for a moment, completely absorbed in cataloguing the state of Miss Adams. She appeared intact physically but despite her still self containment, Ellis would swear she looked injured in some way. He supposed it was an injury of her spirit. But how was he to tell that? She looked nearly exactly the same as she had the night before when they hadn't been properly introduced.

Lucy stood to do the honours. "Sean, I think you might have met Miss Bastion and Miss Adams last year, did you not? But Lord Severn, you may not have been introduced."

There was a flurry of activity as everyone murmured their greetings and shook hands. Ellis lingered over Miss Adams' hand longer than was strictly polite, but he couldn't help but get lost in her gaze as her eyes met his when he clutched her hand. It was as though he were frozen for a moment, bent over, hovering, not quite brushing his lips over the beat that fluttered in her wrist. He couldn't read the thoughts in her intelligent gaze. But he wanted to. It was the oddest sensation.

"Ellis, why don't you take that seat with Miss Adams and tell her about your scents." Lucy's amusement was clear in her tone, but she didn't reprimand him for his uncharacteristic lingering.

The young woman's startled laughter was a comfort to him somehow so he didn't even care if it might be at his expense.

"Your scents?" she repeated in a low voice. "Is that what you were telling me about last night? Your extraction processes?"

Ellis grinned. "Exactly correct," he praised. "Thank you for remembering."

"I thought it sounded fascinating when I wasn't certain what you were talking about, but if it's related to scents, that sounds even more interesting but still rather confusing."

"Perfumiers need to extract the oils from different plants and substances in order to mix their properties and create unique scents. That is what I've been working on. A way to speed up the process and increase the output."

"Oh, that sounds impressive," she said with bright eyes and a breathy voice, as though she were full of admiration. Ellis felt his chest expand much like a strutting rooster on a farm. It was ridiculous and yet marvelous all at once.

"I could show you," he offered. "If you come out to the estate," he added when he remembered suddenly that they were in London and he had left most of his equipment at home.

"Perhaps one day," she said, her tone dying into one with far less enthusiasm.

"Mr. Smythe will be working with us on the business side of things," Lady Evangeline stepped into the conversation, directing her words to Miss Adams. Ellis could feel a frown tugging his eyebrows together.

"Will you be involved in their affairs?"

It wasn't likely the best way of phrasing his question, he realized as pink tinged her cheekbones and she shot him a startled expression, which she quickly recovered into a pleasant smile and a nod.

"It will be a bit of a stretch for the poor woman, she is likely to be run ragged for at least a fortnight, but she is going to do her best," Evangeline interjected once more, examining Ellis with her shrewd gaze. "Perhaps you will be free from time to time to assist, as well, my lord, if you don't return to your estate too quickly."

A start of guilt assaulted him. His estate. He wasn't sure if Lady Evangeline was referring to Severn or the Alldred place where the Northcotts had set up the Scholarly Society but whatever she had meant, he really should visit his own estate one of these days. He did his best to look after it but considering that it may or may not remain his, depending on Uncle Beaverbrook's progeny, Ellis had very mixed feelings about the property.

He could feel Miss Adams' watchful, intelligent gaze upon his face. He wasn't sure what she might be able to read there, but prickles of embarrassment assaulted him between the shoulder blades. He had allowed too long to pass without comment.

"We needn't trouble his lordship," the lovely woman said with a gentle smile. "I'm certain I will be able to assist you however you might need."

Ellis was fascinated by the conflicting emotions that struggled across her face before she smoothed out her expression. It was as though she hadn't meant to say what she did. As though she didn't mean to commit herself or perhaps, she didn't intend to speak at all. She had given him the impression she was extremely self-contained so perhaps it was that final possibility. She appeared surprised to have spoken. What a fascinating creature. She was like one of the botanist's little wood creatures that Lucy never wanted collected. Still and silent for fear of being noticed and, in turn, harmed.

Just like with the little creatures, Ellis felt an urge to comfort the woman and assure her he would never harm her. But they were in the withdrawing room of Everleigh House with several interested people staring at them. It would be ridiculous to create more drama than necessary. And it wasn't likely to make the woman feel more comfortable.

Instead, despite his aversion to the liquid that Lucy swore solved all ills, Ellis asked for a cup of tea.

Lucy's eyebrows lifted toward her hairline but she didn't comment, merely asking "one lump or two?" Since he always refused the brew, she wouldn't know how he liked it. He didn't know how he liked it. In fact, he was well aware that he hated it. But perhaps sugar would make it better. "Two, please," he said with a twist of his lips that closely approximated a smile.

He was certain Lucy was laughing at him, but she kept it nearly hidden. Thankfully the others in the room weren't as aware of his usual staunch refusal to touch the drink so there wasn't any other comment. But he now had an excellent excuse to take his seat and listen to the rest of the conversation.

Miss Adams didn't contribute to the conversation often but when she did, it was always insightful. Ellis had to admire such a trait. She would make an excellent scholar, he thought. She would be of great assistance to Lady Evangeline. Eve had chosen wisely if she did in fact need a companion. Perhaps she could keep the woman on as an assistant even after she wed Sean and didn't need to have as much care to her reputation. It seemed the little companion would be at loose ends and would be an excellent addition to the lady's household.

"Should we take the women to see the house?" Sean asked Lady Evangeline.

"Oh, that probably isn't advisable for another day or two," Evangeline answered. "It's still upside down with workers and their dirt."

Sean wrinkled his face over this news. "How long is that likely to take?"

"It has only been two days since we even got the keys," she answered with a laugh. "How quick did you think it would be?"

"He's just anxious to wed, I would think," Roderick explained with a chuckle. "It's perfectly natural."

"There's hardly a need to rush," Evangeline protested before her gaze met that of her fiancé. "Well, we might hurry, but there are certain things that need to be arranged before it could possibly be feasible. And well you know it," she added firmly to Sean who was making sheep's eyes at her. "Be a part of the solution, not part of the problem," she added with a laugh.

"Surely I am being a part of the solution," Sean protested.

Ellis was happy to see his formerly serious friend acting lighthearted and seemingly happy. He thought to divert everyone's attention to something less fraught than marriages and business affairs.

"Would anyone care to offer their opinion on my latest scent?"

"Did you bring your potions with you? You had best make sure you don't stink up Everleigh House or we'll never be allowed to return," Lucy admonished with an easy-going laugh.

The others were supportive in various ways although Roderick and Sean were less than enthusiastic in their nods, and Miss Bastion and Miss Adams appeared more confused than he expected. Miss Adams, though, despite her confusion over his words appeared intelligently interested as he tried to explain the process and what he had been looking for in the elements of the scent in an easy, non-scientific manner.

Her nods and bright, watchful gaze made him feel as though he were inventing something of immense importance.

He supposed, given the poor hygiene of some of their peers, creating pleasant scents was an important task. But while that was the means by which he intended to bring in the wealth he wished for, he also intended to use his extraction techniques for medicine and other less lucrative needs that would fulfill his urge to help others, not just himself.

He had found the perfect source of income for one such as him, if he did say so himself. Now he just needed to figure out the rest of his life. It took valiant but diligent effort to prevent his gaze from straying toward the pretty companion at that thought.

Marriage was not on his syllabus just yet, he reminded himself.

Chapter Seven

Adriana was fascinated with all the intelligence floating through the room. It would seem she and Miss Bastion were the only ones who weren't doing something noble with their lives. Miss Bastion appeared to be fascinated with the people in the room, not necessarily the topic they were discussing. But Dria didn't mean to judge the woman. That was really quite expected in their circles of association. She had never before met anyone who discussed such intelligent matters.

While it was true that some ladies enjoyed discussing literature or even politics, no one she knew had been sufficiently educated to be able to experiment safely with chemicals and compounds to the point of being able to create pleasing scents.

Ought she to be ashamed that she never considered how her rosewater was acquired? Adriana had always thought she had an inquiring mind. Or rather, she had used to have, when she was a student with Mary. They had loved reading and learning, and they each worked hard to best the other during tests and examinations. But that had been sisterly competition added in to the curious minds of children.

It was a little disconcerting to realize that the pressures and disappointments of adulthood had closed off that youthful curiosity. Well, it had for her and Miss

Bastion, but it didn't seem to be true for the others in the room. She now understood what had been meant when they said the Northcotts had a scholarly society. She saw now that they truly were scholars, studying various topics and striving to invent new things or improve upon old ones.

"Shall you need an investor?" Lady Evangeline was asking, bringing Dria back to the present rather than the depths of recriminations she seemed so skilled at finding.

Mr. Northcott and Viscount Severn both laughed. "We are hoping to manage without one," Mr. Northcott said.

Lady Evangeline nodded. "More profits that way, of course. But if you find you need one, please consider me as your first choice."

Adriana blinked, shocked to realize what was being said. They were going to make a business out of the work Lord Severn was doing. She was oddly disappointed but then called herself to task. She would do the very same thing. She herself was anxiously looking for any opportunity that would afford her a greater income. That was why she was even sitting in this receiving room that day. She was about to start being the paid companion for two women at once. It was rather lowering to realize that the others were going to be helping her achieve that goal without recompense. Ought she to offer to pay them when they were to accompany Miss Bastion in her stead?

Heat filled her. She wasn't sure if it was embarrassment or shame. But she was the only one in that room who was in service. Mrs. Northcott was going to accompany Miss Bastion as needed as a favour, not as employment. It was a distinct difference.

But Adriana didn't have the luxury of choice, and she refused to contemplate the fact that she was lower on the social scale than the others in the room. She was in no position to be disappointed in Lord Severn for wishing to turn a profit. And it would seem that Mr. Northcott was somehow involved in that pursuit as well. She would be interested to learn more in the days in which they would all be at Everleigh House.

The conversation swirled around her and she tried her best to remain attentive. Miss Bastion hated it when Dria allowed her attention to drift. But their visits were often deadly dull. That was not the case this day so she had no excuse at all.

"How soon would you like to collect your things and take up residence here?" Mrs. Northcott asked Miss Bastion.

Miss Bastion cast an expression bordering on frantic at Adriana. It was easy for her to interpret. The woman would dearly wish to remove immediately but she wasn't sure if that was in poor taste. Adriana nodded and offered her a gentle smile.

"It will likely take us a day or two to arrange for our things," Adriana murmured softly. A flicker of disappointment crossed Miss Bastion's face but she nodded and actually offered a slight smile that Dria thought might be one of gratitude.

"We could send footmen to assist you, if you'd like," Mrs. Northcott offered, making Adriana wonder over the urgency of the matter.

Her feelings must have displayed themselves despite her usual impassivity for Lady Evangeline quickly interjected. "Don't be alarmed, it isn't an emergency or a disaster if you cannot join our household immediately. We would just be happy if you could. As you already witnessed, Mr. Smythe is eager to get on with things. And I have much business to conduct. I am realizing a companion would be of particular use at this time."

Adriana looked at Miss Bastion for confirmation. She was well aware that her employer would love nothing better than to join the Northcott household immediately. Dria had thought it wouldn't do to appear too eager, but since their hostess and her new employer both seemed to wish it to be as soon as possible, there was nothing for her to do to stand in the way even if she didn't feel the least bit prepared for this development. But she swallowed her fears and concerns and doubts and everything else and offered Miss Bastion another slight nod.

"We appreciate the offer of assistance. A couple of sturdy footmen would be of great use with our trunks. If you were to lend us a parlor maid as well, we could likely have ourselves together in a matter of hours rather than days," Miss Bastion said to the room.

Adriana couldn't argue the truth of that. Since they travelled frequently, they were accustomed to packing. They could even manage to do it without the added assistance. They had done it often enough with just Adriana and one maid doing all the work, but if she were going to be companion to two separate and unique women, she would have to conserve her energy as best she could and accept the offer of assistance despite the fact that it went against her usual inclination.

"Delightful," Mrs. Northcott crowed. "Now," she said, sitting forward on her seat. "Since we shall all be quite cozy here in the coming days, we really ought to dispense with formalities, wouldn't you say? You must call me Lucy, and my husband is Roderick, or if you'd like to be particularly friendly you may call him Roddie as we do on occasion."

Adriana almost snorted a laugh at this. She didn't know if she could even imagine herself ever being so informal with anyone, let alone the rather austere gentleman. Well, austere wasn't the right word. Dria tilted her head to examine the man for a brief moment. There was nothing austere about him when he looked at his wife. Despite the usual fashion of husbands and wives of High Society living their lives separately from one another, it would seem this youngest Northcott couple had contracted a love match. It was heartening to witness, if Dria were honest with herself. She didn't think it was what Miss Bastion had found for her own future. It wasn't something Adriana had ever thought to wish for her employer. But witnessing the Northcotts' warm affection for one another, she realized it ought to have been. It was a loss for Miss Bastion not to have held out for such a match.

But that woman placed priorities on different things than Adriana did, and she seemed quite content with the match she had made. Perhaps it was purely practical. It didn't matter. The woman was pleased and so Dria would be pleased for her.

She realized the conversation was continuing with the others murmuring their assent to being friendly and informal, at least in the confines of Everleigh House.

Lord Severn was to be "Ellis," Lady Evangeline acknowledged she would answer to nearly any variation of her name, and then Miss Bastion shocked Adriana nearly out of her wits by volunteering, "You may call me Esther."

It took effort but Adriana finally added her own offering. "I am Adriana or Dria, whichever you'd prefer."

It would take getting used to, Dria thought. Even Miss Bastion rarely called her by her given name. No one had done so regularly since her time with Mary. And those memories were wrapped up in complicated emotions she didn't care to revisit. But it might be pleasant to be friendly with people once more. She doubted she would ever go so far as to actually consider any of these people her friends. But friendly would be very nice.

She almost laughed at the hairs she was splitting. She didn't do such a crass thing, though, of course. She merely nodded her farewells as she followed in Miss

Bastion's wake as they took their leave of their new house mates and went to arrange their affairs.

"Send one of the footmen back for the carriage when you are ready and we will come to collect your things," Lucy was saying as they followed her to the door. "A hired hack is likely to go astray and then where would we be?" she asked with a laugh and a gentle wave of her hands.

They were nearly back to their rented rooms when Miss Bastion finally spoke. "Thank you for agreeing to this, Adriana. I know it wouldn't have been your first choice if you'd really had one. And I'm sorry that you likely feel that you didn't have a choice."

Dria opened her mouth to reply but then there was nothing to come out. What was she to say to that? Miss Bastion carried on.

"I know you are better trained in what is proper behaviour than I am, and you have been wonderful about catching me before I do something I'll regret. I will miss your presence beside me when or if I go about with someone else from Everleigh House while you're occupied with Lady Evangeline. But I'm thrilled, positively thrilled, at this opportunity. I swear I won't let you regret it. I will make sure you have the perfect, well-paying position when I wed and when Lady Evangeline is finished with her need of you. It seemed to me that Mr. Smythe was more eager than most bridegrooms, so they may not have need of you for long. But I know you worry about your family, so I will make very certain that you are taken care of just as you'd like."

"Thank you, Miss Bastion, I appreciate that," Adriana finally choked out.

She did appreciate it. She didn't speak of her family often, but it was a constant source of anxiety for her. It was the only reason she was in this position in the first place. But she would be better able to face the coming days or weeks with Miss Bastion's promise ringing in her ears.

Anxiety made everything more challenging. It would be unnerving trying to be companion to two women at the same time. If she had anxiety pressing down on her at the same time, she wasn't likely to be able to do it.

Now she could breathe. She should have known she could count on Miss Bastion, but since the woman hadn't promised to help her before and had in fact seemed reluctant to discuss Adriana's future employment, she hadn't dared to count on any assistance with the challenge.

Lady Evangeline, too, had offered her assistance, but since that was such a new acquaintance, though, Dria wasn't sure how reliable the offer would be. It was something to consider.

But she would still send the letter she was halfway through writing to Mary. It was high time she reached out to her old friend anyway. It was cold and heartless that she had allowed this long to pass since they'd last communicated. It would be lovely to know how the girl went on.

But for the next two hours, she had her work cut out for her.

Thankfully, since they travelled so frequently, she had it down almost to routine. She knew exactly how to pack in such a way that nothing would be in too much of a mess by the time they reached their destination. And that was true if the move was across town or to another country. Any longer than a minute or two and clothes would crease. So, they needed to pack as though they were going to the Orient even though it was merely to Mayfair.

The maid and footmen Mrs. Northcott sent to assist were very competent and before Miss Bastion could become bored and plaintive, they had completed the task.

Adriana had taken the time to speak with their landlady after she had helped the maid get started on the tasks. They had already paid for the next week and a half but had yet to give their rent for the following month so Miss Bastion was quite delighted by the entire procedure.

Mrs. Holland was disgruntled about their leaving, but Adriana assured her as she took her leave that they had been perfectly comfortable in their rooms and she was certain the good woman would have new tenants within a day or two. And it was likely true. Mrs. Holland must have known that or she would have put up a greater fuss about their departure. She would make a tidy profit from their departure in that case, getting a week of rent doubled.

Adriana didn't begrudge it to the woman. She had been a pleasant soul and had weathered life's trials while still managing a fairly pleasant demeanor. Not all their landlords or landladies could say the same. Her time with Miss Bastion had seen plenty of moves and change of tenancies. It was one thing she did not enjoy about her position. Perhaps she would next find employment with someone with their own home. That would be much more comfortable.

Miss Bastion had the means to buy a house, Adriana was certain. But she had such an itch to travel and move about. It was one of the reasons Adriana worried about the woman's upcoming marriage. Viscount Droitmuir didn't strike her as the sort who would wish to travel at a moment's notice.

"Do you think his lordship will mind our removal to Everleigh House?" Adriana asked quietly as they settled into the carriage for the ride back.

She was exhausted already and only hoped she could find a moment to rest before any other duties were thrust upon her. That was likely a pipe dream, but she still made the wish nonetheless. Even if she didn't believe in wishes.

"Why would he mind?" Miss Bastion asked with a frown, recalling Adriana to the matter at hand.

"It might be odd for him to call upon you while you are in residence at Everleigh House."

"Oh, I think he will be most pleased with the association," Miss Bastion replied, her tone taking on an almost preening note, as though she had arranged a great treat for everyone and ought to be praised. Adriana would have snorted if that weren't so terribly low class. She wanted to ask why Miss Bastion would think something so daft, but she held herself short. It was entirely possible the woman knew the man far better than Adriana did. Well, that was more than possible, it should be a given. She just couldn't fathom why a gentleman would want his soon-to-be wife to be cultivating relationships elsewhere. What could he have to gain from it? And should Adriana be worried for her new acquaintances?

Her loyalty was owed to Miss Bastion, of course. But now she had loyalties owed to Lady Evangeline as well as the Northcotts, who were taking them in and offering to assist with Miss Bastion. She swallowed the nervous agitation that threatened. She would have to worry about it all later. They were drawing to a stop in front of the grand house, really almost a palace, that was Everleigh House.

She needn't have been concerned that their presence was an imposition. It didn't appear there could possibly be a shortage of space even if Mr. Northcott's entire family chose to take up residence. It must be a dreadful headache to keep up with the running of such a place. That thought brought her to mind of Lady Evangeline's Spring Street house. What would it be like? Would Adriana have to learn to run it? Was it anything like Everleigh House?

Swallowing down the panic that threatened once more, Adriana admonished herself to take deep breaths. She would be out on her ear if she had a fit of the vapours on the first day in their new situation.

"We shall dine unfashionably early this evening as some of us have commitments this evening," Lucy said as she escorted them to their rooms. "Have you two committed yourself anywhere this evening? If not, you could accompany us or remain here and have a quiet evening if you would prefer."

Adriana hoped wholeheartedly for a quiet evening in, but she knew that was less than likely.

"We accepted an invitation to a rout at Castlemore Place this evening," Miss Bastion answered. "So, an early supper will be most welcome."

"Excellent," Lucy declared as she swept them into their suite of rooms. Adriana was delighted to note that they had adjoining rooms with a small chamber between where their maid could sleep. "Your maid seems most efficient. She is already at work and you shan't have too very much to do to settle in, I dare say."

Adriana dipped a small curtsy and turned to assist the maids. Miss Bastion left the room on Lucy's arm, leaving those in service to do the work. Dria didn't resent it in the least. She preferred not having the woman hovering and trying to tell her how to do it. She was rarely right in her suggestions and it was so much faster if they could get it done without her supervision.

Blessedly, with the additional help of an Everleigh maid, they were very quickly done, and Miss Bastion's personal lady's maid was busily readying their clothing for that evening. Dria was able to sit down in a chair by the window and contemplate the new circumstances. It was almost as good as a rest. It would allow her to get her thoughts in order before the ordeal of a large supper party and whatever the evening held.

She didn't have a great deal of thoughts to gather, though, it would seem when she stared out the window.

If she were to be paid twice, then she could afford the luxury of going to visit her family in between positions. She ought to mention it to Miss Bastion, who had offered to assist her in securing a position. Of course, she still didn't really know what she would be doing for Lady Evangeline nor how long that position would last, so planning for a holiday afterward seemed out of place and unrealistic, at least until more was known.

She ought to have a book to read. Or she could complete her letter to Mary. Adriana wasn't used to having a moment to herself. And really, she shouldn't be lallygagging at this point considering she had two employers to keep happy.

With a soft exhalation that could almost be thought a sigh, Adriana got to her feet. It had been long enough. Surely nearly five minutes had passed while sitting in the chair. What a luxury.

She glanced in the mirror to confirm the state of her hair and then went in search of her employers.

Adriana nearly got lost half a dozen times as she made her way toward the withdrawing room where they had all been that morning. She thought that was the best place to start, although perhaps she had reasoned falsely on the matter. It wasn't very likely Lady Evangeline would remain there all day. But it was a likely destination for Mrs. Northcott and Miss Bastion. Or rather "Lucy" and "Esther," she reminded herself with a slight shudder. Such informality was going to take some getting used to.

She hadn't quite made it to her destination when her forward momentum was arrested by intriguing words floating out of an open door.

"The treasure has to be the lost manuscript I'm looking for."

"Don't be daft, Percy, it's surely the lost library of Alexandria."

"Why would it be that, Spence? Surely to be called treasure it has to be gems or gold or some such bauble."

Treasure? Gems? What were they talking about? Were they jesting or was there to be a treasure hunt? Could she involve herself? What a decadent thought, but one she couldn't avoid. She had never been presumptuous or given to fantasy but suddenly her imagination took flight.

It was decidedly bourgeois to stand and eavesdrop on such a mercenary conversation, but Adriana couldn't help herself. If she could get her hands on a windfall of some sort, she could go home and still support her family. If they would have her. She swallowed the lump that formed immediately upon that thought. If they didn't want her, she could retire to Bath or some such place, support her family, and still not have to run and fetch at someone else's command.

No, she was being ridiculous. There was no such thing as lost treasure except in fairy tales. Certainly not for one such as she.

But the strong male voices certainly seemed to think there were.

"What do you think, Severn, you're being awfully quiet."

Adriana started. She hadn't thought that gentleman might be present. She really needed to get away from the door and find her employers. It wouldn't do to be caught dithering with her ear to the door. She retraced her steps as quietly as she could manage and found a servant to direct her. Within minutes she was seated with Lady Evangeline receiving an explanation of the coming days.

But a portion of her thoughts remained in that hallway pondering the possibilities. *A treasure*, she thought again with breathless excitement she tried to ignore.

Fairy tales weren't for her, she admonished herself as she forced her attention to the matters at hand.

Chapter Eight

The other men were being unforgivably foolish for such well-educated gents. Lady Evangeline's treasure hunt was nothing more than a wild goose chase, Ellis was sure of it. While it was true that her late husband was a brilliant businessman and the evidence they were basing their search upon had been found amongst his papers, Ellis was certain that wasn't enough for them to base such outlandish hopes upon. For one thing, there was scant information in the papers that had been found thus far. Ellis suspected it was all a ruse or a misunderstanding. But some of the fellows were absolutely convinced.

"It would be terrific if it was a genie's lamp," he finally said in answer to Spencer's question. The others laughed and one threw a pillow at him but they carried on with their speculations.

"I'm going to follow this clue," Percival declared, pointing to one particular section in the document they had been pouring over. "Wouldn't it be marvelous not to have to depend on benefactors at all? Roderick and Lucy are the jolliest of fellows and I don't want to leave their estate, but wouldn't it be better if it was our estate, not theirs? We could buy into it and all share in all the profits, not just the ones who land on a lucrative deal."

"Is that really what you want? You're sounding like a socialist or a revolutionist."

"Not a socialist, a utopian," someone else said with a guffaw.

"Nah, not utopia, and not a commune. Just a little more equality than what we have now," Percy said with an emphatic shake of his head. "I would still want to pursue my ideas and hope one of them takes off, but there would be a little less pressure. Maybe the ideas would flow better that way."

"Not me," Ellis said with a chuckle. "I've always found the pressure helps."

"What do you know, anyway? You always have Beaverbrook's pockets to dip into," Spencer taunted.

"Maybe. Unless he finally gets a son," Ellis answered quietly, intending it as a jest, but not quite achieving that if the sympathetic glances he received were anything to go by.

He could understand why their imaginations would be caught by the possibility of a treasure, but it wasn't the most logical pursuit for a group of scientists. While it was true that there were documented treasures that had gone missing, many of the things the different men hoped it might be, in fact. But if the mathematician were in the room, he would surely tell them the odds of their finding it were remote at best. Even if they had supposed clues found in Lady Evangeline's late husband's papers. If that mercenary man hadn't found it, what was the likelihood of these fellows doing so?

His thoughts must have been echoed in the thoughts of the others for Percy piped up again.

"Come on, men, we're well educated scientists and engineers. If we can't figure out a treasure hunt, no one can. That's why Lady Eve's husband didn't find it. He might've been good at business, but not necessarily investigation. Not like scientists."

He wasn't wrong, Ellis thought. There was truth to the words. They bandied around some ideas for a little while longer but then Ellis had to bow out. He had too many other things on his mind between his extraction equipment and what exactly he was missing to perfect it as well as worries about his young cousins and their father's endless pursuit of a son. He wanted to stay in Town to support the scholars' efforts at helping Lady Evangeline and Sean, but he would have to check on Severn soon.

And then there was the little companion.

She intrigued him. There was no avoiding that truth, either. He couldn't put his finger on what it was about her that was so fascinating. He had met plenty of beautiful women in the past. Intelligent ones, too. But it was her stillness, and her compassion. An odd combination. He could tell she didn't want to be there, but she was trying very hard to hide that fact and make a go of the commitment now that she'd agreed to it. He had to admire that in anyone, but especially when found in a pretty young woman. Ellis suspected it was rare.

Not to say that he didn't know other women who stuck to their commitments. His aunts had certainly done so. Right up until their deaths, poor souls.

He really needed to check in on his cousins, he reminded himself once more. If Miss Adams weren't so occupied, he would appreciate her advice on their behalf. Perhaps he could ask her anyway. She wouldn't have to visit the girls to be able to give him a few suggestions of how to help them, surely. Of course, if she met them, she'd be in an even better position to do so, but that wasn't realistic at this point, he didn't think. But he would ask her at supper time.

As was always the case, the clock made its inexorable way around and he had the opportunity to speak with Adriana quickly.

They had assembled to await the butler's instructions and there was only Miss Adams, Miss Bastion, and one of the scholars quietly standing about when Ellis entered the room.

"We are the early birds, then, I see," Ellis called to the room as he approached.

"Good evening, my lord," Miss Adams greeted him with a brief curtsy.

"I thought Lucy said we were to all be friends," he admonished.

Her blush was becoming and she smiled slightly but she didn't amend her words. Perhaps next time.

"Might I ask you for some advice, Adriana?" he asked, emphasizing her name slightly, making her colour rise even brighter.

"Certainly," she replied immediately but without using any form of address at all. Ellis smiled, amused at her avoidance techniques.

"Are you familiar with the ways and thoughts of young girls?"

She blinked at him, surprise evident on her features before she quickly smoothed them into what he was coming to recognize as her usual expression of polite interest.

"I was once one, so I suppose we could say that I'm somewhat familiar."

Ellis smiled. "No governess experience, then?"

"No," she said, shaking her head. "I do have a sister who is fifteen, but I haven't spent time with her at this stage, we merely communicate through letters, so I am far from an expert." She paused as a furrow formed between her eyebrows. "Might I inquire as to why you are asking?"

Ellis sighed. "I have seven cousins, they are all sisters, my uncle Beaverbrook's daughters."

"Gracious. That must be a lively household," Adriana replied with a light laugh.

"It is, for certain, at least at times. When my uncle isn't there in particular."

"Oh," she said. The one small note giving voice to the fact that she could clearly understand some of the situation. "What would you like to know?"

"I don't even know what I don't know, to be honest," Ellis said, exasperation bubbling under his collarbone. He shouldn't have started this conversation, he realized. How could it possibly end? "I would like to help the girls in some way, but I'm not certain how I can do so. They may be my responsibility one day. Or they may not. But they are still my cousins, members of my family, and I care about them."

"Of course, you do. It is kind of you to even think on it."

Ellis' heart squeezed. He appreciated her confidence in him. But what he really needed was assistance. He didn't think she was going to offer it. She had gone completely still and he thought her attention had drifted.

"Have you listened to what they have to say?" She asked it quietly and in a hesitating way, as though she were afraid to ask, like it might offend him. But she asked it anyway, and she stole a piece of his heart in that moment.

"That's a very good question. And I can't say that I really have. Thank you, Adriana. I will take some time and ask them their thoughts."

The smile she offered him was as though moonbeams had lit up the room. He felt as though he were the wisest man on earth in that moment. But it was her. She made him feel like he really could solve all the problems he and his cousins faced. Whether or not he was Viscount Severn. If he could get his extraction process perfected as he knew he would. It wouldn't matter if he had a title. He could help his cousins no matter what.

Supper was announced but it passed in a blur for Ellis as his thoughts centered on his need to finalize his experimentation. Perhaps he ought to return to the estate. Lucy wouldn't appreciate it if he had any experiments go wrong in their beautiful London house.

Chapter Nine

Adriana was overwhelmed with all the information Lady Evangeline had shared with her. She didn't know anything about business or investments or banking or properties or shipping or mining. It was lowering to realize how little she knew about so many things of importance. But Lady Evangeline didn't expect her to know any of it. She herself was learning most of it as she went along. She just needed Dria's company. But Adriana was determined to learn.

And then the handsome chemist asked about his cousins. Or rather he asked Adriana how he could help his cousins, which in a certain way was one of the sweetest things she'd ever heard. But on the other hand, why would the intelligent man have started with the very basics? How could he ask her about his cousins when he hadn't even asked them about themselves?

It almost made her laugh but that would have been insulting to the poor man. He was just being a rather typical man, really. He thought he knew all there was to know, so it didn't occur to him to start with something so basic. But the expression that had crossed his face when she had pointed it out had been one of gratitude, not anger, for which *she* was truly grateful. He seemed much struck by the thought and Adriana was certain he would ask the girls directly how he could be of assistance to them at his earliest opportunity.

Adriana's heart hurt for the girls. She didn't know them, of course, but considering what she had heard about Lord Beaverbrook trying to have a son to replace Lord Severn as his heir and how many girls there were told her enough to hurt for them. It wasn't likely their father was overly interested in their thoughts either. But now Lord Severn would take the time and for that she was pleased.

If only she could get the gentlemen to discuss their treasure hunt. But she had no idea how to bring up a topic that she wasn't supposed to know anything about. Confessing to eavesdropping wasn't likely to endear her to anyone.

"What have you gentlemen been occupying yourselves with in Town?" she finally thought to ask the table at large. "Have you brought your scientific endeavours with you or are you using this time as a holiday from your work?"

Dria was rather proud of herself for the question. It showed interest without being nosy and was open-ended enough that anyone could say anything and she could still possibly find out about the treasure hunt.

"No science is allowed in Everleigh House," Lucy declared with a laugh. "It has to be a blanket rule or we would appear to be playing favourites," she explained when Adriana's expression must have displayed her surprise.

"Some of the gentlemen could do much of their work here, to be honest, with more resources for research closer to access. But no experimentation is allowed in Everleigh House. Not since someone started a fire."

"That sounds like a wild tale," Adriana said in a mild tone that produced deep chuckles around the table.

"He was trying to create a forge in his fireplace. It wasn't terribly successful," Ellis explained, gesturing to one of the fellows she hadn't yet spoken with beyond their initial introduction.

"I don't suppose a fireplace would get hot enough to be successful," Adriana said, nodding. She was flustered by the warm approval she could see in the viscount's eyes. Heat flooded her chest but she didn't linger on the sensation. There was nothing to come of it. If she were to form an attachment to the fine gentleman, all that could come of it was a dalliance that would ruin her. She firmed her features and made every effort to harden her heart. Her family needed her. Heart flutters were not for one such as her.

"What does everyone specialize in?" she asked after there was a slight pause filled with the scraping of cutlery on plates as the assembled guests enjoyed the production Everleigh House had put on in its dining room.

The gentlemen went around the room naming their sciences.

"Astronomy."

"Cartography."

Lady Evangeline's fiancé looked up from his beef to grin. "I'm an engineer, a mathematician, an economist, and I'm about to become a trader or some such. I might need Spencer's advice on ships and such since his specialty has had him on the seas for years."

"Gracious," Esther said, looking up from her beef. "You are all so dedicated, aren't you?"

It was a rather odd thing to say. Even Adriana couldn't tell if she were criticizing or commending the gentlemen. Thankfully the scholars seemed to take it in stride and Adriana turned the topic back when none of them had a comment to make over Miss Bastion's words.

"What about you, Roderick?" she asked, uncomfortable with the use of his name but determined to follow the directions she had been given. "Everyone seems to look to you as the chief scholar, what did you specialize in?"

His chuckle was warm but she sensed discomfort in it from him, and Dria regretted singling him out with her question.

"I specialized in studying," he answered her with little hesitation. "I could never settle on a specialty. My passion was just all knowledge. I didn't have the thirst to build or invent or really niche down to a conclusion like these fine fellows. But I seem to have the bourgeois skill of seeing how their studies could be made into businesses. So, I am the one responsible for finding backers and bringing their ideas to the public."

"Is that how you got to know Lady Evangeline?" Adriana asked what she thought was a simple, innocent question but it brought laughter to the table that confused her.

"I do hope to be one of their backers," Lady Evangeline answered. "But I actually came to them seeking help to discover if I might have a sufficient competence to become independent. I sought the mathematician."

"And you certainly gained him," Spencer called out even as he stuck his elbow into Sean's ribs with a chuckle.

Sean and Evangeline exchanged a glance filled with such affection that Adriana had to turn her gaze away so as to not be swept with jealousy. She was happy for them, she told herself. It just wasn't a state for her.

Adriana turned her attention back to the fascinating topic of the gentlemen's studies. "What is the most surprising thing you've discovered?" She thought it would be interesting, whatever their answers, but she still hoped they might bring up their discussion of the treasure.

"I think I might have found some new stars. They are new to me, but I'm trying to ascertain if it's just that I didn't pay enough attention in class," the astronomer concluded sheepishly.

"That's interesting. How could you have possibly found a new star?"

The man shrugged as though it wasn't anything a great deal. "I made a stronger telescope. It makes it so you can see even more clearly than before."

She nearly gasped with her admiration and the man couldn't help but preen under the attention. "You can see for yourself some time," he offered.

"Is it at your scholarly institute?" she asked, slightly disappointed by the thought as she would never be able to travel there under any circumstances that she could imagine.

"I brought one with me, in fact," the astronomer returned with a quick glance at Lucy to see how she was taking that news. "It's not an experiment, Lucy, it's just looking through a telescope. I'm not breaking the rules, I swear it," he explained almost petulantly before he turned back to Adriana, an eager listener. "The only trouble is, it's almost always too cloudy with all the factories belching out their smoke every single day of the week. But if there's a clear enough night, I'll show you, if you'd like."

"Oh, that would be most delightful, I'm sure." Adriana wasn't completely sure what it would be like, in all actuality. She was nearly always tired when they were in Town with the hours they kept. But she did long to see stars. It was so rare that they had the opportunity whether it was because of light interfering or the hours they kept, or the wretched clouds always about. But it would be delightful, even if she had to prop her eyes open to enjoy the experience.

"I would like that too," Esther volunteered, surprising Adriana. She offered her employer a smile, a sense of guilt sliding up her neck over having seemingly monopolized the conversation. A good companion blended in with the woodwork unless conversation needed to be stimulated. She had nearly forgotten her place. And she hadn't managed to get anywhere in her quest to learn more about a possible treasure hunt. If there even was one. It was entirely possible the gentlemen had been jesting or discussing something completely unrelated to what she thought she had heard. Perhaps even something one of them had read somewhere.

But it hadn't sounded like that.

Adriana resolved to look in the room outside of which she had heard them speaking. There was the very slightest chance something remained that would tell her more. If she could find her way back to that room, she thought with a slight frown. It was a very large house.

She wasn't able to give the matter much more thought that night as they had to hurry to tidy themselves after the meal before making their way to the rout they had promised themselves to.

Dria was in company with Miss Bastion that night as Lady Evangeline had a full entourage to accompany her and had accepted another invitation in any case.

Under usual circumstances Adriana quite enjoyed a rout. The variety of entertainment and the slightly less formal bearing of the event lent itself quite nicely to conversation and being a little more comfortable than usual. But these weren't usual circumstances. She felt pulled in seven different directions and had the uncomfortable sensation that she was constantly in the wrong. It was not pleasant.

"Have you seen Lord Philips?" Miss Bastion asked her.

"Not yet, have you had word from him today?"

"No. I sent a note round to him by one of the footmen, letting him know about our change of circumstances but I had no word back from him."

Adriana glanced sharply at her employer. "Are you concerned?"

Esther waved her hand as though to dismiss Adriana's question. "Not at all. He mentioned he would be happy about any such development so there shouldn't be anything to bother me."

Adriana tried not to frown but how could they have possibly surmised such a development would come about?

"Is it unusual that you didn't hear from him?" Adriana didn't think so. The man didn't sit in Esther's pocket despite their commitment to wed. But it was odd of her to have raised the topic, as well.

"Not in the least. But seeing how Roderick and Lucy behave has made me a little wistful."

Adriana nodded. One couldn't help a slight pang of envy seeing how happy the couple appeared to be. "And Lady Eve and her swain, as well."

"That one is much stranger, don't you think? Mr. Smythe isn't even proper *ton,* so I don't know what she is thinking to make such a misalliance."

"He has been accepted everywhere, I thought," Adriana pointed out gently.

"I can't understand why. It was the only cause for a degree of hesitation over their invitation to take up residence at Everleigh House. I couldn't see how it won't besmirch my reputation to be in the same residence as that one. But it's Everleigh, and he seems to be welcome there, so that sort of reconciled me."

Adriana blinked. She had been in company with Miss Bastion long enough to understand how the woman's mind worked. Or so she thought. She knew the woman had toadying tendencies but she hadn't thought she was a complete snob.

"Do you think it will bother Lord Philips?" Adriana wasn't sure where Miss Bastion was going with her concerns and she didn't really wish to entertain them but she did want to understand.

"I don't expect so, he's an experienced gentleman of the *ton* after all." She answered airily making Dria wonder even more why Sean's parentage would be of any concern to Esther if it didn't bother anyone else. "It might encourage him to hurry along the date of our wedding, though."

"Would you be glad for that?" Adriana would have thought so if it were her but Miss Bastion didn't appear to be in any sort of hurry to wed.

"I'm nearly ready," she said with a smile that actually lit up her face. "Did I say thank you for accepting Lady Evangeline's rather outlandish proposal? I know it's going to drive you to Bedlam in the short term, but I hope you can get benefit from it. I'm sure you will. Being connected with the Northcotts has to be of benefit to anyone. I will make sure you benefit, or at the very least are taken care of when it ends."

To her shock, Adriana felt a lump in her throat over the other woman's words, even though it was nearly a repetition of what had already been said. It had been a challenge being Miss Bastion's companion these last several years, but she was her friend of sorts and Dria would miss her when their ways parted. She threaded her arm through Esther's elbow and gave it a squeeze.

"I still think you should wed," Esther said seemingly out of nowhere. "All those scholars in the house must be tickling your bluestocking soul."

Adriana smiled. It wasn't a new topic. Since Miss Bastion had turned her thoughts toward marriage for herself, she thought it was the solution everyone should consider. But their situations were not the same and she had grown weary of trying to explain that to her employer. She kept her smile in place through effort of will, not amusement.

"I know, I know, our situations aren't the same, you've told me enough times, I ought to know. But surely, it's time for your family to look elsewhere for their support. You need to think about yourself and your own future one of these days. Who's going to look after you when you need a companion to care for you? That's what a husband and children are for, Dria. To be honest, Adriana, you ought to set a runner to investigate if your family even needs your funds any longer. It's well past time for them to be finished with depending upon their daughter. You really need to find a home of your own."

Again, that pesky lump returned to choke her, and it was even more difficult to swallow this time, even though it was accompanied by a healthy dose of irritation over the other woman's suggestion. Miss Bastion wasn't wrong. It was something she thought about in the middle of the night when her worries arrived to haunt her – worries about her own future. But she couldn't see any other way around it. She had been supporting her family since she was eight years old. It was really all she knew. And surely, they wouldn't be taking advantage of her. Would they?

"Let's get you safely and successfully married off first, and then we can worry about me later," Adriana finally answered, turning Esther's attention away from the sticky topic.

With an uncharacteristically light-hearted laugh, Esther accepted the adjustment and the evening progressed as smoothly as could be expected.

Adriana couldn't help thinking about the possibility of treasure from time to time. Especially after Miss Bastion pestering her about marriage. If she had a windfall that could take care of her family, then she would be in a position to see to herself. Esther wasn't wrong about her desire for children. She tried not to think about it too often, and she really had very little experience with the creatures, but it was an instinctive desire that drew her.

It likely stemmed from a desire to recreate a happy childhood she had never had the opportunity to enjoy for herself. Or rather, to relive the simple, delightful time she could barely remember before she joined Mary's more complicated childhood. Those memories were sullied for her when she found out she wasn't acceptable to be Mary's companion in truth. Dria tried very hard not to feel angry over her family's use of her employment, but it took too much effort in her exhausted state. She needed to find a better solution.

Chapter Ten

"I forgot you were going to be in attendance this evening," Ellis lied with a straight face even as the woman's wide intelligent gaze examined him as though to read his thoughts before a gentle smile stretched her lips and a twinkle reach her eye.

"Would you like us to leave?" she asked, clearly amused rather than offended by his words.

"Not at all," he said quickly. "Might I fetch you some punch or some other refreshment?"

"Oh, do run along and get me a glass, please, Miss Adams," the other woman said with an almost shooing gesture at both of them, making Ellis look at her skeptically.

"She must have spotted Lord Philips," Adriana told him with a sighing sort of laugh that was hard for him to interpret but he took to mean that she was of two minds on the subject.

"Do you not enjoy his company?" Ellis asked with a frown, wondering if he ought to plant the man a facer.

His intent must have been clear on his face as she brightened with colour and smiled but shook her head decisively.

"He is perfectly proper and there's really nothing to dislike about his company."

"Except?"

His one-word question brought another twinkle of laughter to her usually serious face. Ellis quite liked that he could brighten this slightly austere woman with his humour.

"Perhaps it is that I don't care for change and his presence in our lives will quite drastically change mine."

"Because of Miss Bastion's marriage?"

"Yes," she answered simply. "But that cannot be blamed upon the poor gentleman. It is the nature of things and I am pleased for Miss Bastion as she is quite delighted with the turn of events. It is just that she had previously intended to remain a spinster. That had been her clear stance for several years. But something changed this year and she decided it was no longer to her liking so here we are, in Town, with her betrothed."

"And you facing a great change."

"Yes," she answered once more.

She didn't even sigh or wince or complain. It was quite shockingly admirable. Ellis wondered if she was completely natural.

"Have you discussed anything scientific with the botanist?"

She blinked briefly over his very sudden change of topic as they walked toward the refreshment table.

"He did explain to me his field of study, or rather some of it. I'm certain it is far more varied than what he had time to tell me in our brief conversation."

"He is trying to cross plants with each other to create something unique. It is quite fascinating but entirely unnatural. Since I have met you, I have, upon occasion, wondered if someone did the same with you."

"I beg your pardon," she said, glancing at him with an unguarded expression for the space of a heartbeat, her face filled with both amusement and horror, clearly wondering if he were insulting her publicly.

"There is a very snooty cat on the estate who likes to visit my laboratory from time to time. She is quite beautiful but can stare at me for an age without blinking and I can never be sure what she is thinking. You put me in mind of her when you manage to keep all expression from your face save a very pleasant and, I suspect, quite fake, smile that would lead anyone to think you hadn't a single thought in your pretty head."

She stopped in her tracks, forcing him to do the same, and stared at him blankly for the briefest moment before a chuckle seemed to overtake her.

"I will take that as a compliment, my lord, thank you," she finally said quite pleasantly and set off toward the refreshment table once more as though nothing untoward had been said. Inexplicably, his admiration for her grew.

"You are the most compelling woman I have ever met," he murmured to her as they accepted the glasses of punch from the maid serving it and turned back toward where they had left Miss Bastion.

"But you have been at school for most of your life, have you not, my lord?" Adriana returned with a pleasant voice and a sweet smile. It took him a moment to ascertain her implication. When he did, he nearly guffawed aloud in the crowded hallway.

"You imply that I have met few women and therefore don't know what I'm talking about?" he asked her with laughter still evident in his voice. "You are forgetting that as Viscount Severn, I have been called upon to circulate amongst my uncle's peers from time to time for years."

"But have you actually spent any amount of time in conversation with many women? I dare say I am far from unique."

"I would argue the point but that would hardly be polite, would it?"

Her eyes twinkled at him when she glanced from beneath her sweeping eyelashes toward him for a moment and his stomach actually fluttered with unnamed impulses. He knew he was in trouble then. Beaverbrook would never approve of the woman. She was barely gentry. She was beautiful, intelligent, well spoken, and graceful, really everything a Society woman ought to be. But the Earl of Beaverbrook was such a stickler, he expected his heir to match with a social equal at least, even if he were to be disinherited.

But what did he care for Beaverbrook's opinion? Ellis had resisted his uncle's efforts to match him for the last two years, surely he didn't really care what the man thought. And if he weren't to remain the heir, all the less should he marry someone who would end up dissatisfied when she was demoted from viscountess to Mistress Dorval at some future date.

"Might I call on you?" he asked before they reached Miss Bastion's side.

This question didn't seem to make much sense to the woman walking beside him. "Whatever do you mean? We are staying at the same residence for the time being. We are likely to meet in the breakfast room. Why would you need to call upon me? Have you been sniffing too many of your chemicals and compounds and your memory has been affected?"

She asked that last question with laughter sounding in her voice, as though she were jesting, but he could see genuine concern in her features as she frowned up at him.

"I meant to say, could I take you for a drive or a walk or some such?" He really meant to ask her if he might court her, but he didn't really wish to spell it out quite so precisely in the crowded room.

"That is kind of you, Lord Severn, to be sure, but considering my current situation there is very little likelihood that I will have even five minutes to spare in the foreseeable future, let alone the hour or more that such an excursion would require. But I do thank you for the lovely thought."

With those pleasant but dismissive words, the woman did just that, it was as though she dismissed him from her mind as well as her presence as she hurried toward her employer with her glasses of punch and without a backward glance toward him to see how he took her words.

Chapter Eleven

W*alking or driving or some such? What was he asking? Did he just ask to court her?*

Adriana was almost dizzy at the thought. Surely she had misunderstood. Or he truly had been overlong with the compounds in his laboratory and had lost his mind, poor soul. As if a viscount would wish to court her. And as if she had the time or the inclination. Well, she certainly didn't have the time. And she didn't wish for the inclination. Even if there were a whisper of temptation niggling at the back of her mind.

It was not for her, she insisted for the hundredth time. Now she had both Miss Bastion and her own mind trying to convince her that a courtship would be a good idea. How could it possibly be?

If she found a treasure, perhaps it would be possible.

She was tossing and turning in her very comfortable but unfamiliar bed at Everleigh House after the rout that night. Adriana wasn't certain how she got through the rest of that event without throwing a fit. Miss Bastion had become more demanding than usual for some strange reason. It was as though she were trying to be unaccommodating despite her wish to change their circumstances. It had taken every ounce of Adriana's considerable control to remain as pleasant and placid as usual.

But she had managed through sheer force of gritted teeth, forced smiles, and her indomitable will. There had been no fits, no scenes, nor even any outward unpleasantness. Their hostess had bade them goodnight with a clear eye and a pleasant tone as she wished them to call upon her at one of her earliest at home days.

Of course, it was possible she was just saying that, but Adriana believed she had been sincere. It was likely Miss Bastion would follow through on the invitation with Mrs. Northcott or some other member of the household as, from what Lady Eve had told her, Adriana was going to be quite busy for the next few days.

But first, she was going to search that room.

The very idea of a treasure was ridiculous. And she was even more ridiculous for thinking she could involve herself in the hunt for it. But she was going to do it anyway. That resolution got her through the night and she awakened earlier than usual but feeling remarkably refreshed, despite the dreadful evening she had experienced the night before, never mind the short and restless night.

Springing out of bed, Adriana quickly dressed, untied the plait she had put her hair in, and redid it into an appropriate daytime style with enough pins to withstand whatever the day might bring, all without ringing for Miss Bastion's maid. They shared the woman's services when needed such as if Adriana needed a particularly intricate hairstyle for certain events or if a gown was a little too challenging to lace herself into, but for the most part, Dria was used to doing for herself. Ever since it had been made clear to her what her true standing was by Mary's guardians, she had been determined to keep her place and remain as independent as possible.

But if she found treasure, the first thing she would do is hire her own maid. That thought nearly triggered a fit of giggles. What a silly goal in life. But silly or not, it was what symbolized, for her, the difference between those in service and those receiving service.

She needed to find a way to search that room first, though.

She didn't want to tiptoe as that would make it far too obvious that she was sneaking, but she also didn't want to draw any attention to herself. She hoped no one else was up and about, but of course the servants would be. She was in a peculiar position in the household. Not quite a servant, but not quite a resident either. No one should really pay her any mind. But she was far too nervous to dismiss the possibility that someone would confront her about what she was doing in that room.

If she could find the room.

The house was so large and had so many hallways and doorways and stairways that Adriana didn't think anything looked familiar. She feared she hadn't been paying sufficient attention the day before when she'd been looking for the receiving room.

Just as she was about to give up and go in search of the breakfast room, which she could comfortably ask a footman for directions toward, she found what she thought must have been the small salon in which she had heard the gentlemen discussing the treasure.

Small salon was probably a misnomer. It wasn't really small. But were any rooms in this very large house? Not even the dressing room between her and Miss Bastion's bedchambers could rightly be called small.

But the salon was the smallest public room she had yet seen in the lovely grand house, a fact for which she felt immense gratitude as it would make it easier to search.

Should she shut the door? Should she scramble around looking on any available shelf? *What had she been thinking when she thought this was a good idea?*

Just when she was about to turn away, though, she saw a sheaf of papers on a small desk in the corner. This was why those gentlemen had assembled here. For one thing, it being a small, out of the way room made it less likely they would be disturbed or disturb anyone else. But the available desk was also probably a draw for the scholarly gentlemen.

If there were going to be any notes about treasure in this room, that is where it would be, Adriana told herself as she brought the door nearly to a close and then strode purposefully toward the desk. She would quickly look through the papers and then she would be on her way.

Shock nearly made her gasp aloud. The top sheet of paper appeared to be a list written out in very tidy handwriting. At the top of the page was the stark heading "Treasure" and then an enumeration of what looked like clues the writer had gathered. After her initial shock resolved itself, she almost burst into laughter. Was it a jest? Was someone playing a trick on her? Had they spoken aloud in the hopes she would hear and pursue a futile chase?

None of the scholars she had met struck her as being particularly unpleasant or cruel so she shouldn't suspect them of setting her up for a fruitless search. She doubted they could have possibly been aware of her overhearing them in the hallway. So, this would prove that someone believed there to be a treasure. And that someone was preparing to search themselves.

But what were they searching for? From what she had overheard, it didn't seem the gentlemen were even sure themselves what the treasure could be. But it was somehow tied to Lady Evangeline's late husband from what she was reading on the papers in her hand.

The details were scant. Adriana nearly seethed with impatience. With the situation and with herself. Was this any of her business? If it was connected to Lady Evangeline, could it be argued that it was Adriana's duty to involve herself? Or was she meddling where she didn't belong?

The idea of treasure was enticing, she could understand why even the scientifically inclined scholars were intrigued. She was more than intrigued. Treasure of any kind, even a small something, could change her life immensely.

She was hooked. She needed to know more.

Adriana wished there were some way she could make a copy of the notes. Perhaps she could steal one sheet of paper and quickly jot down a few notes. She would have to take care not to disturb anything nor leave any evidence behind herself. But this would give her plenty of food for thought later. Until she could decide if she ought to bring it up with Lady Evangeline, at any rate.

It felt like far too much time had passed and the loud ticking of the clock on the mantle nearly drove her mad as she wrote as much and as quickly as she could. A sound in the hallway brought her up short and she froze with the pencil in her hand, bent over the desk with what she suspected was a wild expression on her face.

It must have been one of the maids going about their business, but it reminded Dria she must be on her way. Quickly folding the paper and putting everything back where she thought it had been when she arrived, Dria slipped her notes into her pocket and hurried toward the door. Smoothing a hand over her hair and cheeks hoping she didn't look too wild-eyed or harried, she opened the door in a manner that she hoped didn't appear to be one of guilt nor of subterfuge. She stepped into the hallway and tried to remember if the door had been ajar or closed when she'd come across it. It must have been ajar, surely, or she wouldn't have recognized the room. She thought that made sense but she couldn't be certain.

She almost bit a hole in her lip in her indecision. A puff of laughter propelled her away from the room without looking back. It didn't matter. Even if it wasn't exactly how the last person had left it, it was a busy house, there was no way someone would become suspicious over a slight difference. If they were going to be so possessive of the contents of the room, they would have locked the door.

That reassurance comforted her as she turned down another hallway, far enough away from the room she had searched to be able to heave a sigh of relief and be comfortable to approach a servant for directions to the breakfast room. She was almost certain she would have been able to find it on her own but at this point she was hungry, confused, and anxious to be settled somewhere that didn't feel sneaky.

The room was wafting with delicious odors as though the staff had just set up the food, so her timing was perfect. There were already a couple of the gentlemen present. She was the only female. She hadn't thought of that. Should she have had a tray brought to her room? It was a bit late for that now and it wasn't something she was used to. It was often her preparing their meals and bringing a tray to Miss Bastion. She had never availed herself of that luxury except when they were travelling and staying in a hostelry in which she wasn't comfortable. And then it hadn't felt luxurious, it had felt as though she were trapped. This was luxury. Choosing what to put on her plate while the food was still warm and delicious looking. In a hotel, it was extremely rare that she ever got pleasantly warm food brought to her room. Coffee or chocolate might be warm when it arrived, but she usually settled for toast as it was difficult to ruin that. Possible but difficult, she thought with a slight smile and forced her feet to propel her into the room.

Hovering outside was going to make her look foolish and that was about all it would accomplish. It certainly wouldn't feed her.

And she wasn't about to be ruined by eating breakfast in the breakfast room of Everleigh House even if it were occupied by only gentlemen. The plural would surely save her even if there were a possibility of impropriety.

But it was Everleigh House. No one would even consider claiming the possibility of impropriety. Surely.

She was making herself mad. She needed to eat.

"Good morning, Adriana," Viscount Severn called to her followed by murmured greetings from the other occupants of the room while a footman hurried forward to assist her. It would seem the chemist was following Lucy's instructions about informality to the letter. Heat touched her cheeks.

"Good morning," she paused, hesitating over his address. She ignored her discomfort and the awkward situation. She didn't have to say any name. In fact, saying names was odd. Would she then have to address each of the occupants of the room directly? No, a general good morning would suffice for everyone. She hadn't eaten yet. Conversation could come later.

"Did you sleep well?" Ellis persisted. Clearly, he was a cheerful sort in the morning. She usually was too but she had already caused herself anxiety by her search *for* the room and then her search *of* the room. She needed to eat before she could be pleasant or cheerful or even really anything approaching personable. She put a bite of meat into her mouth hoping that would be sufficient excuse for not talking.

Ellis laughed. "Not a morning person, then," he said in a droll tone. "Very well, I can mind my quiet for a few more minutes."

She wasn't sure if he could, but he at least turned his conversation to one of the other gentlemen in the room rather than expecting her to converse. A lively discussion ensued about the stars visible the night before.

"It's the dang factories, Severn," the astronomer complained. "There's barely a light visible any night in this city. I'm surprised anyone even knows there's a moon in the sky if they've only ever lived in London. We're lucky we grew up in the countryside or we'd likely never even have gone to school."

"Chemicals work wherever you live," Ellis countered with a slightly pious tone making the others laugh and Adriana smiled over their boisterous talk.

"Not true," the sailor called. "I climbed a mountain once and things didn't work nearly the same as they do at sea."

Adriana listened to their banter and bickering, smiling over the rim of her cup at their easy interactions. It was obvious the men had been friends a long time.

"Have you all been together long?" she finally asked when there was a brief lull in their conversation as everyone applied themselves to the contents of their plates.

"Since we were boys at Eton," Ellis said with a grin. "Most of us, anyhow. Some are different years, of course. Any who weren't at Eton with us, we collected at Oxford when it became obvious we weren't just there to fulfill some family tradition."

Her frown must have shown she didn't know what he meant, so he explained.

"Most only carry on to Oxford as a social event or because their family expect it of them. Large families have their heir and their spare and then any more sons are sent to school to become clergy. Some of us just loved to learn." The other gentlemen were nodding and laughing, mentioning some of their friends who hadn't been as scholarly. Ellis continued, "Roderick was one of the exceptions. He being the youngest, his father didn't have any enforced expectations of him, he just loved to learn and wasn't sure what else to do with himself so he stayed at school. When Adelaide, his oldest brother, you know, ribbed him about it, Roderick vowed he would stay at school until he had read every book in the library. And do you know, I think he actually managed to do it. But then he got the idea to start our Society and finally left the school to buy his estate and wed with Lucy and he brought the rest of us with him."

"Were you all staying at the school until you had studied everything?"

"Our families thought so," laughed one of the others.

Ellis shook his head, though. "Most of us were still there on grants or sponsorships from others who had expectations of our studies."

Adriana frowned. "What does that mean?"

"If your sponsor wants you to study salt, you study salt," Ellis said with a grimace.

"I suppose that happened to you?" She was torn between amusement and horror on his behalf.

"Only briefly, but yes."

"And he's one of the luckiest ones. With his title and allowance, he didn't really need a sponsor." The one who said that sounded only the slightest bit envious.

"I had to use my allowance for repairs that quarter," Ellis explained.

"That's why Sean switched to maths when he lost his sponsor. Old Charlie wanted him to be an engineer but when he couldn't invent what Charlie wanted, the bounder moved on to someone else."

"So, do you mean, if he had invented whatever was expected of him, it wouldn't have benefited him?"

"Oh, it likely would have to some extent, it usually depended on what sort of contract had been signed. But most of us didn't know anything about contracts or hadn't even bothered. We just wanted to keep studying. So, Roderick saved us. Of course, the old fellow will benefit some if one of us comes up with something truly brilliant, but he isn't taking advantage of anyone. And he lets us all pursue what we want, not what he thinks is going to make him the most heaps of money."

"He did suggest I adjust my pursuit," someone else pointed out grumpily.

"But that solved the problem you had been grappling with for months," another gentleman pointed out without sympathy.

Adriana laughed along with the rest of them.

Chapter Twelve

Ellis watched the companion hurry from the room when the clock had struck the hour. Apparently, she had an appointment to keep. He had enjoyed her presence and her intelligent gaze as she'd followed the scholars' conversations throughout breakfast. He suspected she had understood most, if not all, of what had been said, at least after she'd asked a clarifying question. It wasn't often he found women even showing an interest in most of what the various gentlemen were pursuing.

His perfume extraction device was one of the rare exceptions, of course. But Miss Adams had seemed to take an interest in all of the scientists and even the cartographer. It had been heartwarming and very attractive.

Which was a disheartening thought. Even though he had asked her to step out with him the previous night, it was a good thing she hadn't understood what he was saying. No matter how attractive she might be, he really wasn't in a position to pursue a courtship.

He needed to get his own house in order before he could consider filling it up, he reminded himself, mixing his metaphors a little, but it well illustrated that he didn't need any more complications than already presented themselves between his uncle's antics and his invention's complications. But an interested and interesting female was hard to ignore.

A grin stretched his cheeks.

"Seems Severn is smitten with the newest addition to the party," someone called out.

"First Smythe, now Severn? We should have known Roderick's marriage was going to be dangerous for all of us."

Good natured laughter filled the room before Percy shrugged and said, "There's something to be said for having a partner, though, don't you think? You can't tell me either Roderick or Smythe are unhappy with their fates."

There wasn't any more laughter after that and the scholars quietly left by themselves or in pairs, likely to go back to their rooms to read or to leave in order to gad about town.

"I'm thinking of heading back to the estate," Percy said. "I don't think Lady Evangeline needs our help anymore, and I can't get anything really productive done here in the city."

"Can we even go back there with Roderick and Lucy here?"

"Why not? They said it's our home too."

Ellis nodded. It was probably a foolish question. He had just come to think of the lot of them as his family. Like they were a unit of sorts. But that was probably just wishful thinking on his part. Look at Sean Smythe. It wasn't likely he'd be returning to the estate at all if he was going to wed the wealthy widow and help her run her businesses. He seemed immensely happy with the mathematical challenges that were before him. Ellis laughed. The man had wanted to study economies. He had been thinking of nations or municipalities. But it would seem the man's betrothed had more wealth than that. It should be exactly what the man had wanted.

And the best part was, in Ellis' opinion, the mathematician didn't even covet money. He just loved numbers and the study of commodities and economies and how that all worked together. It was a beautiful match for the wealthy widow. She didn't have to fear that Sean was after her money and yet the man was going to delight in helping her manage it.

If only he could find someone like that for himself.

Ellis rolled his eyes. He was being daft. He didn't need the complication, he reminded himself. Sean was free and clear to divide his attentions with a wife. Ellis didn't have that luxury at the moment. And it didn't matter if there were a fascinating woman under the same roof. She had her own concerns to deal with as far as he could tell. He wouldn't want to interfere with what she was going to be doing for Lady Evangeline in any case.

And now here was a servant with a message for him written in Uncle Beaverbrook's decisive scrawl.

Severn,

Meet me at my club this afternoon. Might have a new marriage on the horizon.

Beaverbrook

Ellis sighed. His uncle wouldn't stop in his pursuit of an heir. And that was perfectly within his right, of course. Except that he had already basically killed two women in his headlong pursuit as both his wives had died in childbirth. Ellis was surprised the earl could find another woman willing to make the attempt with him but he supposed the title and everything that came with it could be highly attractive to many young women.

For it was surely going to be another *young* woman. Beaverbrook was convinced that the younger the better for birthing a healthy son.

Ellis had lost count of how many pregnancies and infants the previous countesses had lost. Poor souls, his thoughts turbulent as he tried not to be emotional on the topic. But all those lives had been members of his family for however short a period of time.

He truly didn't begrudge his uncle's pursuit. It was inconvenient, of course, as it left everything unsettled in his own life. Ellis had always known, even as a young boy, that while currently he might be Viscount Severn, that could always change if Lord Beaverbrook fathered a son. Pregnancy after pregnancy had caused uncertainty in his life. Every child who'd survived had been a girl. Ellis wasn't sure about the others. He wondered what his friends studying anatomy would make of the situation.

It didn't matter. Well, it mattered, of course. Ellis had been raised to think of Severn as his, or mostly his, and Beaverbrook as potentially his. He had been taught to love the properties, their tenants, the land, and all that went into them. But he had also gone away to study. Besides devoting himself to Beaverbrook, he had known that there was a very real possibility it would never be his, so he had also pursued other interests.

His brother was the lucky one. Their parents had focused on him and his prospects, an old aunt on their mother's side had left Lucas an inheritance that let him lead the life he wanted with a small property and a competence. Lucas was comfortable and settled, sowing a few wild oats in Town from time to time but mostly living a bucolic life in the country. He was a year younger than Ellis and almost ready to be a settled family man with his recently affianced wife to be and a comfortable future in front of him.

Ellis was still straddling both possibilities. The impoverished scientist or the wealthy, land owning earl. Which was it to be? Both brought their complications. Either would satisfy him. Both satisfied him now in a certain way. It was disturbing to be waiting on someone's death, though. If his uncle would just sire a son, then the waiting would be over, and Ellis would get on with his focus on profiting from his science and being a distant relative to the Beaverbrook family.

For now, though, he would have to see what his uncle had to say. And he was resolved to check on the welfare of his cousins. Whether his uncle liked it or not, those girls were still his family and needed to be provided for with more than just governesses. Ellis hoped the new stepmother might actually take an interest in them. Someone needed to.

He chose to walk to the club. It wasn't far and he was used to the exercise. Despite hunching over chemicals and burners most days, Ellis was well aware that he needed movement every day or he'd end up stuck in a bent position.

Of course, Beaverbrook thought it was lowly to walk.

"You should have taken a carriage," he complained as soon as he caught sight of his nephew. "Didn't you buy that phaeton I suggested to you last year?"

"No, my lord, I decided I didn't want to waste the ready. And it wouldn't do me much good considering how little time I spend in any city anyway."

With a humph the earl settled himself into his chair. "Out on that estate with all the other mad scientists of yours. You should have left that all behind years ago, Severn," Beaverbrook grumbled.

"If you would settle one way or the other on the matter of heirs, I could do likewise," Ellis pointed out as politely as he could considering the number of times they'd had this particular conversation. "Tell me about your new countess," he invited.

Beaverbrook didn't appear terribly enraptured with the subject change. "She's not my countess yet. Negotiations are still ongoing."

"What seems to be the trouble?" Ellis asked with a frown. Despite his headlong efforts to father a son,

Beaverbrook didn't appear to be unhealthy, dissipated, or mad. He was getting older, it was true, but he still seemed fit. And the family coffers were large and well filled from what Ellis knew from his last quarterly visit with the stewards and solicitors.

"Her father is a little concerned about the deaths of my first two wives."

"Concerned in what way?" Ellis asked with a frown. There had never been any whisper of a suggestion that his uncle was involved in any wrong doing. Of course, it could be said that he was fully to blame considering the poor women died trying to provide an heir.

"They want to stipulate how often I can get her with child."

Ellis stared at his uncle. "How could that be stipulated?"

Beaverbrook found one of his rare smiles. "You do know how these things work, don't you, my boy?"

Despite his embarrassment over his uncle's jest, Ellis merely smiled, shrugged, and nodded. "I have studied the matter, in fact. And I understand the logistics, but I wonder how anyone could enforce such a demand."

"Well, as a matter of a gentleman's word, I suppose. You're right, no one could really enforce such an agreement, but if I agree, I will abide by it. It would be my honour at stake, you know."

"So will you agree?" Ellis asked. It was a reasonable demand, in all actuality. He had to respect the family members who had asked for it.

"I will continue my search a little longer to see if I can find someone as suitable with fewer demands," Beaverbrook said before shaking his head and shrugging. "To be honest, though, there aren't many more prospects who will have me. It's a tricky business, Severn. Most of the potential brides are barely older than my own daughters. That doesn't seem quite right, does it?"

"Have you considered a widow or even a spinster?" Even though his uncle was trying to have him replaced in the succession, he was still his uncle, his father's brother. Ellis owed the man his respect and he actually liked him at times. The part of him that was determined to solve problems couldn't help but make the supportive suggestion.

"I have considered both, actually. Widows especially. If they have a son, that would bode well for me, don't you think? But most don't want to be bothered, especially not if they are already well-placed in Society. I'm not the prospect I once was," he said with a despondent sigh.

"Do you think perhaps you ought to accept what Fate has decreed and just see to enjoying the time you have left with your daughters?" Ellis asked the question as gently as he could but wasn't sure if he had succeeded when the man's face flushed with anger mingled with determination.

"You'd like that wouldn't you?"

Ellis sighed. "Not necessarily, my lord. I will admit to you, the uncertainty is irritating. I love the lands. But I also love my studies, so I shan't be left with nothing to do if you do sire an heir. But I worry for my cousins."

"You are free to do with them what you will," Beaverbrook returned with an all-encompassing gesture making Ellis' eyebrows rise.

"Really, my lord? You wouldn't mind if I stick my oar in with your daughters?"

"Why would I mind? There are so many of them. It would be a blessing to have them bleating to someone else other than me from time to time."

"Perhaps your new wife will want to take them in hand."

"If she isn't much older than they are, it will be a mite challenging, wouldn't you say?" Beaverbrook asked, obviously without actually wanting a response. "But she needs to be focused on other things, not the girls."

Ellis' mood soured over his uncle's heartless words but he resolved to go forward with his intention to see what he could do for the girls. It was likely he was to be their guardian if something were to happen to his uncle whether there was a boy child or not. He really ought to have seen to them before now. But he wouldn't abuse himself over the matter. He would just start as soon as possible.

"So what did you want to discuss with me about the potential bride? Isn't that why you wished to meet with me?"

Beaverbrook sighed. "I really wish you weren't so likeable, lad. I want to feel justified in my determination to supplant you. With you being so personable it feels like I'm being an idiot to try so hard to have an heir of my own loins."

Ellis laughed and shrugged. "My apologies for being a gentleman," he said. "Some of the blame can be laid at your own doorstep, you know. I have been meeting with you every quarter for more than a decade."

"True, but it's your parents who made you who you are, I can't take any credit considering how I've resented you. I still do, so don't take this as acceptance of your existence."

"I would never be so bold," Ellis returned, needing to exercise effort to maintain a straight face.

"You're a scallywag, Severn," Beaverbrook grumbled with half a grin. "You've helped me decide. I will accept that girl's terms, Severn, and I will do my best to replace you," Beaverbrook declared. "But you *will* see to all your cousins, won't you, even if there's a boy?"

"Of course. That is one thing you did teach me, Uncle. I feel a very strong sense of obligation toward both Severn and Beaverbrook. Even if neither is mine, your children will still be my family. I will do my best to care for them even now, while you are still present."

"Very well, you're a good lad," the man agreed, knocking back his drink. "Wish me good fortune, Severn, I'm off to woo a wife."

Thankfully his uncle didn't wait for a reply, merely striding away with Ellis staring after him. He swallowed hard. He did wish his uncle good fortune. Unfortunately, they had differing views on what that was. Beaverbrook already had seven healthy children. He had lost at least that many in the meantime, besides. In Ellis' opinion, the man ought to be satisfied with what he had. If he wanted a wife for partnership, companionship, and assistance with his daughters, Ellis could completely understand that, but this compulsion to sire a son, while he could understand it in theory, in practical terms, it was leading to more trouble and death than it was surely worth.

And then there were his own prospects. He really tried not to be selfish about it. Beaverbrook was entirely within his rights to want a son to inherit rather than a nephew. But as the nephew who had been raised as Viscount Severn, Beaverbrook's heir, it was disconcerting to try to be Severn while also making arrangements for a different life should the need arise.

Perhaps the treasure the fellows were talking about searching for was a good idea after all, especially if it were gems as some of them claimed it must be. While he truly hoped to finalize his extraction process and gain his independence in that way, he was a scholar who quite firmly believed in covering all the possibilities. He certainly wouldn't say no to a little treasure falling into his lap.

With a nod, he too got to his feet and made his way to the door. He needed to return to Everleigh House and figure out some things for himself.

Chapter Thirteen

Adriana thought her hand was going to cramp from all the notes she was taking.

"I think that's it for now, thank you so much, Adriana, this has been exceptionally helpful."

Dria offered what she hoped was an agreeable smile to her second employer. "How do you know all these things?" she finally asked.

Lady Evangeline laughed. "I have just learned them myself. I now have solicitors and stewards and managers and clerks all running around doing things for me and providing me with lists and reports and information. It is very overwhelming, as you are finding out. It should come around to making sense soon. I am already getting it straight now, at least some of the things. You will catch up quickly, I can tell."

Adriana wasn't so sure but she didn't want to discourage her employer from thinking that, so she merely nodded. "What else can I do for you now?"

"Lucy is looking after Esther for the day and quite excited about that, so if you aren't too worn out, I would appreciate your company on a few errands."

"Of course," Adriana replied immediately. Her own fatigue didn't matter. Besides, she wasn't actually that tired. She could shake it off easily enough.

"Before we run off, I could use a cup of tea. Would you like one too?" Without waiting for a reply, Lady Evangeline rang for a servant and within moments there was a steaming pot before them. While they had waited, Adriana had spent the little bit of time straightening up the papers she had been going through and familiarizing herself with the rest of Evangeline's paperwork. She thought some of it might be similar to what she had found in the scholars' room, making her think, once again, about the possibility of treasure, but she didn't have a chance to question it before the other woman was asking her something.

"Might I be so impertinent as to ask you how you came to be in company with Miss Bastion?"

Dria swallowed her sigh. She wasn't sure how to explain her situation without seeming like she was complaining. She really didn't have a complaint about her life. But she did hate to appear pitiful. She pinned a smile to her face and launched into her tale.

"My father was somehow acquainted with a gentleman named Mr. Gerald Leverett. I believe they had gone to school together as boys. Unfortunately, my father took ill when I was very young and was no longer able to support our family. We were never High Society but we could have almost been considered gentry, or really, we *were* gentry, just on the fringes of Society. Both of my parents have distant cousins who are connected to the *ton* in various ways. It was never very clear to me, but because of that, I can be considered acceptable."

"I would say for more than just those reasons, but never mind, carry on," Lady Evangeline said kindly and in a gentle tone that somehow made a lump form in Adriana's throat.

"Yes, well, when I was almost eight years old," she continued, after clearing her throat, "Mr. Leverett came and offered my father a way to support the rest of my family. He had just become the official guardian of another one of their old school chum's daughters. She was a lady. A very young lady. And an heiress, of course. But she was lonely. And her guardians determined that she needed a companion to grow up with. So, I became her sister of sorts. I was too young to understand the arrangement, of course. But I remained with Mary until she turned seventeen. It was then determined that she needed an older companion to chaperone her as she took her place in Society."

"She would have been very young to make her debut."

"Yes, she didn't much enjoy it, from what she said in her letters."

"And then what became of you?"

"Mr. Leverett, after explaining my real situation, fortunately didn't just throw me to the wolves. He found me another position, this time with Miss Bastion. Mr. Leverett was connected with her through the management of her inheritance, if I understand the matter correctly. And I have been with her ever since."

"And is your family still taking advantage of your employment?" Lady Evangeline's voice was steady and even, but there was a note in it that indicated to Adriana that she didn't quite approve of that arrangement.

"What else were they to do?" she asked, trying not to squirm in her seat. Dria could hear the defensive note in her own voice and tried to hide it but couldn't quite manage to conceal her discomfort.

"You were a child, Adriana. Your parents should have been providing for you, not the other way around."

"Children even younger than I was go to work in factories every day."

"That may be true, but that is hardly a defence, my dear. That is even more disgusting, but only marginally so. You were a child, and a gently reared one at that. No child should have to work to provide for their parents. And it shouldn't have continued to this day. What about your own future? Are you the only child? Do your siblings also have employment and support the family?"

"No," Adriana answered quietly. "Well, that is to say, my brothers do, now that they have finished school."

"So your responsibilities toward them should, at the very least, be lessened if not curtailed entirely."

"Perhaps so, but if I do not mind, then I don't see how it is really of your concern."

Adriana truly didn't wish to offend her employer. As she herself had pointed out, she needed to be in service in order to support the others. But she didn't know how to defend the decisions that had been made, and she didn't know how to change the situation. Perhaps Lady Evangeline was correct and it wasn't right that she was being expected to support the family. But she needed to be needed, and her family needed her. So, it could be said that supporting her family made her happy. At the very least it gave her purpose. And she refused to allow anyone to take that away from her.

If she found the treasure she was trying very hard not to wish for, she would give up her obligations toward the family. Or rather she would once and for all fulfill her obligation. Until then, she would work as hard and as much as was needed, as there was nothing else for her to do.

"Perhaps I should allow Lucy to match you as she truly wants to do."

Adriana laughed a little at the change of subject. Or perhaps it wasn't really a change of topic. It was more of her ladyship trying to run her life. Everyone wanted to run Adriana's life. It had been that way since she was born. Why should she expect it to be any different now that she was an adult?

"What do you mean?" Dria finally asked.

"You may have already heard some of this. But as I understand it, Roderick Northcott wanted to start his scholarly society to support his scientist friends. For that, he felt he needed to marry an heiress. Being a scholar himself, apparently, he made a study of the matter and had a list of potentially appropriate brides. Lucy was seemingly not one of the qualified ladies, but she managed to make him fall in love with her all the same. Now they are blissfully happy, but she feels that she stole a march on everyone else on that list and feels compelled to make certain they are happy. I was one of those. Now I'm betrothed."

"Well, I certainly wasn't on his list."

"No, but I suspect your Miss Bastion might have been."

"Perhaps, but Lucy needn't worry about her, Miss Bastion is very contented with where her life is taking her with Lord Philips."

"Is she happy, do you think?" Lady Evangeline asked, evidently not certain on the matter.

"She would say so," Adriana replied firmly. Happiness wasn't really something most people discussed. She didn't think most even gave it a great deal of thought. She wasn't going to start troubling herself about Miss Bastion's happiness. At least not overmuch. She had that woman's day-to-day affairs to worry about.

"Well, in either case," Lady Evangeline carried on briskly as though they hadn't taken a strange detour into discussing Miss Bastion's potential happiness. "I think we ought to allow Lucy to concern herself with your future. It will be far more entertaining for me, at the very least."

Adriana took a deep breath as a way to control the urge to be angry with the woman. "Is that to be part of my role as your companion, then, my lady," she asked in a controlled voice. "To be your entertainment?"

"I do think it sounds like something that a companion would do, do you not?" the lady asked before chuckling. "No, you goose. Or rather, I do actually think entertaining me is part of the role, but no, I do not expect you to *be* my entertainment. Now get off your high ropes and drink your tea."

Adriana tried to act as naturally as possible, but she was feeling unsettled from reciting her personal history. She so rarely told it. Almost never, in fact. She even tried not to think of it. But it was hers, and it was the truth, and there was nothing much she could do about it. Perhaps she should have made up a better history for herself years ago. But she had still been too young and distressed when she had joined Miss Bastion to be able to make something up, besides the fact that Mr. Leverett had known Miss Bastion's former guardians and had likely passed along her history to them. Since she hadn't changed positions since then, it hadn't occurred to her to come up with a better history. This position had landed in her lap with such suddenness that she hadn't taken a moment to think about telling her tale.

Now it was too late for the relationship with Lady Evangeline. But going forward she would think of some other way to tell it, even if she had to tell the same basic facts. There must be another way of expressing it. One that didn't bring ire from the listener. If Adriana wasn't angry about the situation, she didn't see why anyone else would be. Perhaps it was Lady Evangeline's fault.

What a novel concept. Adriana was so accustomed to taking the blame for anything upon herself that it had never occurred to her that she ought to consider someone else could be at fault in something, especially something like their own feelings.

Her history was her history, and it really wasn't the lady's business to be offended about it. Unless she wished to turn her off, of course, but she didn't seem thusly inclined. It was more that she was bothered on Dria's behalf. But if Dria wasn't bothered, it wasn't her ladyship's place to be bothered either.

Her cup rattled as she placed it back into its saucer. She had never had such outlandish thoughts before. Was it the environment of Everleigh House that was causing it? Being with all these scholars thinking and talking about concepts she had never heard of before might have put strange ideas in her head. Or perhaps the chemist had noxious fumes floating through the house.

A smile drifted across her face, and Lady Evangeline inquired as to its source.

"What has suddenly amused you?"

Adriana could hear answering laughter in the lady's voice, as though she were just waiting to be entertained. But how was she to explain her thoughts? She tried to make something up on the spot and was unsuccessful. Nervous laughter bubbled out of her mouth.

"It's a little difficult to explain, my lady."

"Please, Adriana, I thought we agreed to be informal when we weren't in company."

"Very well, Eve, I allowed my thoughts to wander and they went in an unusual direction. It made me wonder if it was the association or if there were perhaps poisons in the house."

Evangeline stared at her for a moment and then burst into laughter. "And the thought of poison made you smile?"

Dria felt hot colour splash on her cheekbones, but she couldn't help laughing along with the other woman. She lifted a shoulder in a small shrug. "It seemed to be a reasonable explanation. Or rather, not really reasonable, thus the amusement, but it seemed a good explanation for such unusual behaviour on my part."

"And what has been so unusual about your behaviour?"

"Well, nothing, just my thoughts."

Eve's frown indicated she wished to pry further but realized she ought not. Suddenly she laughed again. "Do you know, I will have to agree with you that it is likely the association. This isn't their usual place of dwelling, so I doubt it's the house itself. But being with a houseful of people who regularly question everything does end up having its effect on you. I hadn't put it into words or complete thought until just now, but I certainly changed due to my association with this group. It must be inevitable."

"Well, I cannot change, so I will have to guard against it."

"Why can't you change?"

"It isn't likely anyone will wish to hire a radical thinker as their companion," Dria returned drily.

"Are there other employment options you could pursue?"

"I think a radical is even less likely to be hired as governess, so no, I don't really qualify for anything else. There are lower employment options such as seamstress or certain shops might perhaps consider hiring a female, but those aren't likely to be terribly lucrative."

"No, I suppose not. Perhaps I will keep you on as a clerk after I've wed. You seem to have a knack for this information already. And Mr. Smythe might be more comfortable with our association than if I were to hire a male clerk. But let us leave such future talk for another time."

Lady Evangeline stopped for a moment and appeared as though she wished to say more, but she shut her mouth over the words. A fact for which Adriana was grateful. She didn't want to have to dislike the woman. And that is what would happen if she tried to tell Adriana she needn't support her family any longer.

It was true that with the boys grown, perhaps she should consider cutting back on how much was sent to her family. That would allow her to save some of her income for the future. Mayhap she could even do a bit of travelling on her own before she took another position. It was possible that would be enough of a change to satisfy her and return her to her usual state of contentment.

Ought she to ask the lady about the treasure hunt? It was possible it was a part of her duties. She had seen the matching information. But how to explain what she had eavesdropped upon the previous morning?

Perhaps when they had become better acquainted.

"Do you miss your family?" Dria finally realized that she hadn't asked the other woman anything about her own background.

To her surprise, Lady Evangeline lifted one shoulder in a shrug that appeared rather negligent, but Dria couldn't be sure if it was real or feigned.

"I miss my mother, but she has been gone since I was a little girl, so that is a rather futile wish," Eve finally answered with a gentle smile. "My father became distant and my brother is in a different world, so there wasn't a close bond to miss. I suppose you could say I miss the possibilities or what could have been."

Dria made a sympathetic noise in response. It was rather the same for her.

"Do you see your family often?" Evangeline turned the question back on her once more.

"I haven't actually seen any of them since I left."

"Since you left? Left when?" Lady Evangeline asked, incredulous. "When you were a little girl?" Her previously relaxed posture and expression were suddenly fierce and almost angry. “I cannot fathom how you have survived to be who you are.”

Adriana grew uncomfortable under the woman’s attention. “I am nothing in particular,” she tried to say.

“That is nonsense and well you ought to know it. But never mind. I can see that it might be difficult for you to see it any other way. If you’ve finished your tea, run along and do whatever you might need to do. I would like to be leaving in fifteen or twenty minutes if you think you could manage it.”

“Of course, thank you,” Adriana murmured as she stood, bobbed a slight curtsy, and then nearly ran from the room.

What a disaster, she thought as she walked as briskly as dignity would allow back to her room to ready herself for leaving the house. Had she made things even worse for herself? Why had she not prepared for the possibility of being questioned about her past and the likelihood that others wouldn’t understand?

No one ever asked her. She supposed that was why she hadn’t thought to come up with alternate details about her life. And really, fabrications were not her usual method of communication.

But, oh, that had been uncomfortable.

Bidding herself to shake it off and prepare for the next encounter, Adriana quickly reviewed herself and made some slight adjustments before taking a few deep breaths to steady her nerves and returning to the entrance hall to await her employer.

She was early, of course. Adriana loathed being late for anything that was within her control. Waiting for Evangeline gave her time to contemplate their time together that day. The lady was involved in many fascinating things. It was surprising the woman had hired a companion to assist her, considering Dria’s complete lack of experience in anything similar. But she supposed Eve merely needed assistance, an extra set of hands, as it were. Dria could do that. And she would learn plenty in the process. She only hoped she would be of actual help to the other woman.

And that her reputation wouldn't suffer from the association.

Esther might think the Northcotts' high place in Society would sufficiently protect their associates from censure, but Adriana wasn't so sure. Her connection with the family was of the most tenuous sort. She was loosely connected with a friend of the youngest son. How could that possibly be enough to protect her when Society would wish to criticize her for involving herself in commercial affairs? She, Adriana Adams, was only very distantly related to lower levels of the *ton*. Certainly not enough to protect her from criticism, gossip, or prying.

While Lady Evangeline seemed to be congratulated on her good fortune and the novelty of her taking over her late husband's business affairs, Society wasn't going to rejoice if other women started following in her footsteps. Dria's involvement could very well be a problem for her going forward.

She still didn't know how long the lady needed her services, either. That was a large part of her uncertainty. If the association was brief, it would hardly be noticed. But it left her wondering where she would go next.

"You're worrying again."

Inside, Adriana nearly jumped out of her skin, but on the outside, she barely flinched when the deep voice startled her from her thoughts. She turned to see Ellis lounging against the newel post, apparently about to go upstairs.

"My lord, I didn't hear you come in," Adriana said with a slight frown, which only made the gentleman grin.

"I came in from the mews. Don't tell the butler. He hates such informality."

"It seems quite reasonable, though, doesn't it? Coming around to the front just so the butler or footmen can bow over your hat seems wasteful of everyone's time and effort."

Ellis laughed and shrugged. "I thought so. Which is why I didn't bother. But he can be accommodating and disapproving all in the same breath, so, again, I beg of you, don't tell."

Adriana laughed. "Your secret is safe with me."

"Very well, now tell me yours. What had you frowning so fiercely that you didn't even hear me clatter into the room?"

"Oh," Adriana hoped to be able to airily brush away his question, but she was terribly embarrassed to have been found in such a state and couldn't think fast enough to dismiss him. She really was in a muddle. If only she could take to her bed, but that wasn't a luxury ever afforded to her.

"All is well, thank you, my lord. I appreciate your concern." She finally managed to stammer out a response, but all he could do was laugh at it.

"I thought we were to be friends, Adriana. You cannot fob me off with such weak words."

Chapter Fourteen

The woman's blush was appealing to him in some inexplicable way. It shouldn't be so. Ellis was certain there was a very scientific explanation for the blood pooling in her cheekbones. But the way it warmed her face, and with her eyes downcast in a bashful manner, it just did something to Ellis' chest that was unlikely to be healthful but it was vastly appealing.

And he really did want to know what she was worrying about. Perhaps he could be of assistance.

"I haven't any secrets, my lord," she finally told him in her quiet but firm voice. That same voice that somehow sent shivers on his neck for no reason that carried any logic behind it.

"Isn't it, by definition, a secret if you aren't going to tell me?"

That question surprised a laugh out of her, and he was inordinately pleased by the accomplishment.

"Why would you care what my worries are, in any case?" she asked, her frown returning.

"Every gentleman has as his goal to solve the worries of all fair maidens," Ellis said, bowing with a flourish that brought her back to laughter.

"You are a jester, I see," she said, still not telling him why she had been frowning.

Ellis grew serious. "My dear girl, are you well? Can I not do aught for you? I swear it to you, I'm not a paltry fellow. I could actually assist you with most things."

Adriana's small breath would have been merely breathing on someone else, but Ellis suspected that from her it was a sigh of defeat. He was both heartened and saddened by his accomplishment. He had no wish to defeat the woman.

"I do have worries, doesn't everyone?"

"I would suspect, under the current odd circumstances, yours might be a little more complicated than others."

She nodded in agreement, and Ellis was glad he had persisted. It was as he thought. The poor dear had taken on too much.

"I am just afraid of what shall become of me. It is likely my position with Lady Evangeline is to be very short. And Miss Bastion shan't need me past her wedding day. So, while I am busier than ever at this moment, it could all come to an end within a se'en-night or maybe a fort-night."

Ellis hoped so, for her sake, but it didn't seem as though she were looking forward to being free of obligations.

"Why aren't you relieved?" he asked with a frown.

"Because I need to be employed. And uncertainty gives me hives."

Ellis was surprised into a guffaw of laughter. "Hives, is it?"

She had managed not to even crack a smile over her jest, an impressive feat.

"How can I help?" Ellis finally said and was relieved by the expression of gratification that spread over her features. She wasn't offended by his nosiness, but rather seemed to appreciate his inquiry.

"Do you know anyone in need of a companion?" She knew her tone held sarcasm but really, why was the gentleman even asking. She didn't expect an answer from him. She was just a worrier by nature, it couldn't be helped.

"Well, as a matter of fact," Ellis said as he thought quickly on the topic. "I might know of seven someones."

"You know seven women in need of a companion?" she asked with a frown. Ellis wasn't sure if she didn't believe him or was suspicious of his intentions.

"Did I not tell you about Lord Beaverbrook's daughters?"

"Oh, yes, but surely he has governesses for them and there's likely to be a parade of aunts and cousins excited to lend a hand."

"Surprisingly, and sadly, I suppose, we aren't a very extensive family. As far as I can tell he hasn't arranged for any sort of company for them aside from, as you say, I'm sure there is at least one governess for the younger ones' education."

"Oh dear."

Ellis wasn't sure what her final words might mean, and he really shouldn't have brought it up without discussing the possibility with the girls and his uncle first, but the more he thought of it, the more he realized it was a brilliant idea. His cousins really must be in desperate need of mature companionship. They had each other for company but if no one was putting their oar in to try to offer some guidance, it wasn't likely they really knew how to go on.

Miss Adams might not have a great deal of first-hand experience, never having really made her own debut, but in company with Miss Bastion, surely, she had witnessed a great deal of Society's doings. Enough that she would be able to offer guidance and direction to the girls when needed. And a mature head in the house full of females would surely be a good idea.

He had already resolved to check on his cousins, now he had even more reason to do so. And Beaverbrook had all but told him he could do as he wished with the girls.

"Perhaps I shouldn't have brought it up until I had discussed the matter with them," Ellis said with a downward pull on his mouth.

"No, no, don't let that trouble you, I understand it is only an idea. But I do appreciate your thinking the idea with me in mind," she said with a gentle smile.

Ellis' chest puffed up in a ridiculous manner. And his determination to help the woman increased exponentially, if that were even possible. It was just that it so perfectly dovetailed with his interest in assisting his cousins, he assured himself, nothing warmer than that. With that in mind, he quickly took his leave of the companion and returned to the mews. Beaverbrook hadn't likely brought his daughters to Town with him but if Ellis rode, it shouldn't take him much more than an hour to get to his estate.

His uncle had assured him he would welcome Ellis' involvement in his cousins' lives, so he wasn't doing anything nefarious by calling upon them. In fact, he ought to have done it long ago. It was most unacceptable that he had allowed himself to ignore them and their needs. He couldn't explain why that had suddenly become clear to him only now. He had been in the routine of visiting every quarter. Visiting their father and the estate, of course, but each time he had taken some time with the girls. So why was it only now that he realized they weren't being properly seen to? He supposed it was meeting other women on a different level than he was used to. Social interactions at *tonnish* events were not the same as really getting to know ladies.

The months he had been in residence at the Scholarly Society with Roderick and Lucy were the best of his life since he had begun training to be Viscount Severn and the Earl of Beaverbrook. Being Severn had altered his life in a less than pleasant manner. Oh, he knew he really had nothing to truly complain about, he reflected as he crossed through fields on horseback.

Being Severn had educated him in so many subjects and experiences that surely plain Mr. Ellis Dorval would never have done. But it had added so much uncertainty to his life. Being with the Northcotts and the other scholars had created a firmer foundation than he had felt for more than half his life. Perhaps that was why he was only now ready to turn his attention to helping others.

He would ponder on it more after he had seen them. For now, it was all a rather abstract concept that his friend studying psychology would certainly find highly diverting to dissect.

Ellis made good on his prediction of how long it would take him to reach Beaverbrook. It wasn't much past noon when he pulled up to the stables and threw the reins to a waiting stable hand.

"He deserves a good meal and a rubdown, Pete," Ellis called. "He did very well." The young servant grinned and nodded as he crooned to the cooling horse, walking him toward the paddock to make sure the horse cooled properly before his meal.

With a nod of approval that his animal would be well cared for, Ellis headed for the house where a footman was already holding the door in anticipation of his arrival.

"Lord Beaverbrook isn't currently in residence, my lord," the footman said in lieu of a greeting.

"I am aware. I just spoke with him yesterday at his club, as a matter of fact. Are any of the ladies available for a visitor?" Ellis asked as he handed over his hat to the waiting butler.

The butler's eyebrows rose in the closest thing to shock Ellis had witnessed on the face of the very proper servant.

"All the ladies are in residence, my lord, but they aren't in the habit of receiving visitors."

Ellis wasn't sure what the man was trying to tell him. Did he think it inappropriate for their cousin to visit them? Or did no one know how to go on?

"Ought they be invited to meet me in a receiving room, or should I go see them upstairs?" he asked before adding, "I have come to visit my cousins specifically. Could you please let them know I am here?"

"It is rather irregular, my lord," the butler protested again, weakly.

"There is nothing inappropriate about my visiting my cousins, and I ought to have done so before now so no one would find it strange. You are merely surprised," Ellis pointed out in a soothing tone. "But you needn't be shocked. Send a maid or a footman and see what they would prefer as I haven't a preference."

After another minute of sputtering and conference with a footman, a maid was sent to see if any of the ladies wished to see him. He wasn't left cooling his heels for long when his oldest cousin, Lady Cordelia, arrived at a mad dash down the stairs.

"Ellis, is it really true? You've come to visit us, truly?"

He laughed at her enthusiasm even as he castigated himself for not having done so sooner. From the looks of the girl, she must be already old enough to make her debut. He should have put his oar in before now.

"Truly I have, but I didn't think it would be such a production," Ellis finally answered with a significant glance toward the butler who was still standing by with all the appearance of a disapproving grandfather.

Cordelia waved her hand with a laugh.

"Don't mind Humphries," she said with a wink at the very proper gentleman. "He has had to keep us in order for years, you know. Besides no one ever calls since the last countess died, and never has it happened that us girls have had a caller."

"Shall we change that now, then?" Ellis asked lightly. He would deal with his own guilt later, for now he needed to start looking after his cousins. "Would it be better if you all came down to a parlour or receiving room or should I come up to you?"

Cordelia wrinkled her nose. "How will it affect your dignity to take tea in the nursery?"

"It will be a novel treat for me."

"Well, if you truly wouldn't mind, that would be best for us. Prim and Prue aren't allowed in the drawing room, and it would break their hearts if we were to leave them out."

"We could never do that," Ellis assured her as he offered her his elbow while directing his attention to the butler. "See that appropriate refreshments are brought to us, then, Humphries, if you would."

Cordelia giggled again as she took his elbow. "My Lord Severn, you are turning quite commandeering all of a sudden."

"I apologize that it's my first time, Cordelia," he said in a low, slightly choked voice when they got to the top of the stairs. "I swear to you, it won't be the last."

"Those are kind words, Severn, but wait until you've endured tea with the lot of us before you make any promises you can't keep."

Ellis wanted to protest but then he realized he ought to wait and see, as she had said. She opened the door to an explosion of chaos. It appeared to him as though the room were flooded with noise and movement, but then he realized it was really only the three youngest and a maid making all the ruckus while what appeared to be a very ineffective governess was standing by calling out plaintively for order.

"What has become of you all?" he asked in a commanding voice that brought the attention of all nine females to focus on him.

Equal parts amusement and discomfort flooded him as the silent stares of all nine replaced the bedlam that had filled the room only seconds before. Ellis wondered if he ought to have ignored or even tried to enjoy the chaos, but then Cordelia clapped her hands with a delighted smile and crowed to him.

"Well done, Severn, I have never been able to get their attention nearly as effectively. I think it's the tenor of your voice, don't you?" she asked him with a twinkle in her eye even as she turned to her sisters and called out to the room. "Come around, but gently, ladies, and greet our cousin, Viscount Severn. Some of you have most certainly met him before, but you littlest ones may not have. He has come to take tea with us so best behaviour, please. Won't you try to impress him so he'll come again?"

The silent stares continued for the briefest moment before a quieter chaos erupted once more as each girl wanted to gain his attention. The maid went to stand beside the governess, both of them bobbing him curtsies before stepping back to a corner of the room to observe the situation.

Likely expecting to see me run away in defeat, Ellis thought with grim amusement as he applied himself to trying to keep everyone straight in his mind. He had spent time with the older girls, but he had barely even met the youngest ones.

It was evident they were all related with their similar eye and hair colouring. That was a surprise considering the lot of them had two different mothers. He knew the oldest four were the daughters of Beaverbrook's first wife, Aunt Claudia, if he wasn't mistaken. He hadn't yet been coming for his quarterly lessons when she was in residence. It was only when she had died that his uncle had insisted he ought to begin his training as the heir, Viscount Severn. But if that were the case, then he suspected the oldest girl must be nearly nineteen, since he was reasonably certain he was ten years older than her. She really ought to be making her debut. His second aunt, Patience, had been gone a year now. Surely, they were all out of mourning. Even Uncle Beaverbrook was thinking to wed again, so it ought to be perfectly acceptable for his daughter to make her curtsy to Society.

But she needed a chaperone.

Ellis tried not to sigh as he surveyed the group who were scrambling to arrange seats for everyone, arguing over who would sit next to his lordship as the housekeeper appeared with some footmen laden with trays.

"We never get visitations so this is quite an event for the household, my lord. You'll have to forgive the hubbub it has caused."

"I do apologize. I didn't mean to cause a disturbance."

"Not at all," Cordelia responded immediately. "That was not a complaint, merely an explanation. We could use this sort of disturbance whenever you might feel inclined."

Ellis felt heat claw at the back of his neck with the return of his guilt. But he was here now. That would have to do.

"Would you like me to perform introductions?" she offered in her primly proper voice. Ellis couldn't tell if it was censure or merely restraint making her sound so prim.

"I'm fairly certain I can identify everyone except I might get some mixed up as a few look to be all the same age."

"Yes, some have taken their growth spurts sooner than others. And some of us are fairly close in age, you're quite right." She gestured what he suspected was encouragement to go ahead and try.

"I know Lady Claudia named all her girls similarly to herself with names ending in an A. So there's you, Cordelia, then Seraphina," he started shaking hands as he went. "Lavinia, and Amelia."

This caused an eruption of giggles from the younger girls and consternation to spread on the face of the girl he had just greeted.

"No, silly, that's Penelope," called out one youngster, possibly Prudence.

"I'm Amelia, my lord," piped up a small, delicate looking girl who didn't seem to be bothered by the fact that he had made the mistake.

"Thank you, it's a pleasure to make your acquaintance," he said to both the girls he had mixed up. "And you two must be Prudence and Primrose," he said crouching down before the toddlers.

The one reached over and pulled her sister's thumb out of her mouth. "I'm Prue. And Prim is the baby," Prudence said, trying to sound grown up despite the fact that she couldn't be much more than five or six years old.

Ellis didn't shake his head although that was his inclination. He was certain he would get to know them all well. Right now, they all looked to be versions of each other but already he could see there were strong personalities at play. He was sure they would be a delightful addition to his life. Well, he corrected himself, they certainly weren't a new addition, any of them.

With a smile that he hoped appeared sincere and all encompassing, Ellis gestured toward where the servants had set up the refreshments. "Shall we take tea and get to know one another?"

The youngest girls, especially, quickly scampered to do as he had suggested, still enthralled with the novelty of an adult visiting their small domain, but he could see that Seraphina and Lavina especially appeared reluctant to enter into the spirit of things.

"I suppose I interrupted your activities, didn't I?" Ellis said to them as they reluctantly took their seats after settling an argument about who would sit next to him.

"Cordelia and Sera are the oldest, they will take his sides," Lavinia had declared to the pouting Penelope and Prudence. Seemingly, though, the youngsters couldn't argue with her logic and quickly settled elsewhere. Ellis had never felt popular before in his life. It was a novel experience.

"Some of us like routine more than others," Cordelia finally answered him when it was evident Seraphina wasn't going to say anything.

"I should have sent a note, but I got the idea and didn't want to wait. I do apologize. I will do better next time."

"Be careful about promises, my lord," Cordelia repeated her earlier caution. Ellis nodded, but he knew he would be keeping this one. It was painfully obvious he needed to be involved in the girls' lives.

"Did you see Father in Town, my lord?" Amelia asked, clearly anxious in her small voice and large eyes.

"I did, just yesterday, in fact. That was part of what prompted my desire to see you."

This brought on frowns from some of the older girls. "Did he seem well, my lord?" Lavinia asked with her head tilted as though she would be able to read his mind.

"He did, actually, seem very well."

"He's going to marry again, isn't he?" Seraphina finally spoke. Ellis wasn't sure what her monotonous tone meant. Was that her usual manner of speaking or was she making an effort to remain neutral on the topic?

"It would seem to be his intention, yes," Ellis answered gently, unsure how to handle the subject. "It would be good for there to be a countess to escort you ladies as you make your debuts."

Seraphina huffed a breath that sounded suspiciously like a snort. "As if, my lord. Unless Father times it perfectly, his wife will be in confinement and unable to go about. We have quite resolved that we shan't be going to Town at all."

Ellis stared at the other girls who were nodding along as though in agreement. None of them appeared terribly put out by their resolution.

"Would you prefer not to go to Town?" he asked, hesitating. "I suppose it would be a little daunting to meet the queen."

"We aren't afraid, Severn," Sera blurted out, definitely not in a monotone this time. Her voice was dripping with disdain over the possibility. "We're embarrassed, in actuality. And in practical terms, it would be impossible anyway, unless Cordelia can convince one of the local boys to come up to scratch and then she could escort us."

"Even that isn't guaranteed to work, though, since so few of the gentlemen I even come into contact with have the circumstances to make something like that happen. And we aren't completely sure about our dowries, so I don't know if I even could sponsor the other girls."

Ellis listened with concern to his cousins discussing the matter, even as he tried to keep a matching frown off his own features.

"I don't think anyone should go to London, anyway," Penelope piped up. "We should all stay together forever."

"I know love, and that's likely what we'll do," Cordelia said reaching out a hand to her half-sister before turning back to their guest. "In any case, Severn, you needn't concern yourself with it. If we're content, you needn't be otherwise. Even if you become Beaverbrook, I promise we won't be a burden upon you."

"I would never consider you a burden, but you will be my responsibility. I just recently realized that really, since we're family, you already are, whether I inherit from your father or not. So, I'd like to help if I can."

"As a single gentleman, you really can't do anything in this matter, can you?" Seraphina said this with an almost sneering tone that made Ellis wonder why she didn't just say what she meant. But he didn't know her well enough to ask.

"I can't do it myself, but surely I could find you someone who could. Or help your father find you someone."

This caused the older girls to exchange glances with one another that Ellis couldn't begin to interpret. But he suspected it was mention of their father reminding them that it wasn't likely anything would be done from that quarter.

"As you said, perhaps his next wife will take an interest in us," Cordelia finally said with a note in her tone that made Ellis realize she had terminated the discussion. But he wasn't ready to have it terminated.

"Have you considered hiring a companion? That might do for an escort for Cordelia to make her debut. She might not be able to meet the queen that way, but she could still go about in Town at least a little bit. And I might know a few ladies who would be able to arrange the grander invitations."

"Why are you persisting in this matter, my lord?" Cordelia asked, not in a confrontational manner, but still, clearly uncomprehending.

Ellis looked into her young, but still mature gaze and knew he had been right to come.

"I cannot really explain it to you as I am far from an expert in the workings of the mind, but I have only recently gained a true sense of family from the friends I live and work with. It made me realize that I ought to do more for the family I already had, you lot. And then I realized that since I'm not a youngster anymore, some of you likely aren't little girls anymore, either, and I ought to see what is being done for you. I saw your father yesterday, and he let me know he wouldn't mind if I took a hand with you. I happened to recently meet a woman who is the paid companion to a lady who is acquainted with our society. All the factors combined in my head like a beautiful chemical reaction."

Cordelia laughed while some of her sisters varied in reaction from confusion to scepticism, but none of them objected to his words.

"We shall see, then, shan't we?" was all Cordelia said.

"So, if I can arrange it with Beaverbrook, you wouldn't object? Perhaps two of you could come up next Season."

Cordelia and Seraphina communicated silently once again in a manner that Ellis admired and envied all at once.

"If you could get our father to agree to the expense it is likely to create, then, no, we would have no objection at all," Cordelia finally said before adding with a smile that appeared a little forced. "And we ought to thank you for thinking of it."

Ellis laughed. "You ought to, but you aren't going to?"

Cordelia laughed with him. "Ah, you caught that, did you? I worded it perfectly so that you might think I had been thanking you."

"You've forgotten that I am a professional student. I notice things."

Eyebrows rose around the table from the girls old enough to be paying attention to the conversation.

"That seems to be an enjoyable occupation," Seraphina said as though realizing it grudgingly.

"It is," he admitted.

The rest of his visit with his cousins continued reasonably uneventfully. There was a bit of an upset when Primrose, the youngest, spilled her glass and burst into tears. Ellis suspected she was embarrassed for having made the mistake in front of him, as the youngest girls seemed intent upon being as entertaining as possible. He parted from them after a couple of hours feeling worn out but motivated. He had promised to return.

"I survived. I know what I'm promising," he assured Cordelia who offered him a wide, twinkling smile of approval. "I will send word next time so there is less consternation in the household," he added as he took his leave of all the girls. When Cordelia escorted him below stairs, he added for her ears only. "I will speak to your father about the companion. I think between her and some of my friends, we might be able to launch the two of you into Society with a reasonable degree of fashion."

"I don't care about being high fashion, you know, and I worry about leaving the others. But I also worry about what might become of us if I don't marry." The girl sighed and Ellis resolved to do all in his power to help them. It ought to have been their father's intentions, but he was too focused elsewhere.

"Is it only the wardrobe expenses that concern you? What do I need to know when I speak to the earl?"

Cordelia shrugged and shook her head. "I'm not really certain, honestly. I've never discussed a Season with anyone who knew much about it. Pen, Prue, and Prim's mother talked about her Season with happy delight when she first arrived, but she turned into such a watering pot, I never wanted to ask her about it when I got older. And then she got so depressed about all the babies she was losing. Who could blame her? So, I never wanted to tease her about going up to Town nor even ask about the possibility. By the end, she hardly ever left her room. I did what I could, of course, but our conversations were never about us older girls, only her own daughters and how they went on."

She paused, shifting her gaze away as though in thought. "I actually think the biggest concern might be whether or not he would allow us to take up residence in the townhouse with or without him. Depending on whether or not he does have a new wife and if she were to be in a delicate condition, he certainly wouldn't want to take us to Town. But then he wouldn't likely want us there without him, as it might not look appropriate." The girl sighed again. "I don't know what to tell you, my lord. It's a conundrum that I haven't been able to sort out for a couple of years now. As you said, now that we're out of mourning, it might be doable, but by the next Season, who knows where we'll be?"

"Never mind worrying about it, I'll see what Beaverbrook says when I see him next. We have plenty of time to sort it out, but I don't want to leave it to chance. I'll be sure to put the idea forward and start some sort of planning in motion. If Miss Adams becomes available and your father is willing to hire her, she will be of interest to the lot of you at the very least. And then you'll be sure to be in the right position whatever happens."

As he rode away, Ellis couldn't get the sight of his cousin's face out of his mind. She had appeared to be trying very hard not to have her hopes up but seemed positively delighted despite herself. Her sunny disposition made him all the more determined to do what he could for the girls. He couldn't necessarily say the same for the second sister, the grumpy Seraphina, but she was his family too. He would do what he could for all of them.

Chapter Fifteen

Despite how full her day was, Adriana couldn't stop thinking about the viscount's last words. Could they be friends? Was he really going to be able to find her a position with his cousins? Seven girls? How could she even begin to manage that? She was having enough trouble keeping up with two very different women.

Of course, seven sisters would be a different matter than two such vastly different women heading in quite different directions in their lives. But not by that much, considering there were seven of them.

Surely the treasure was a far better option.

But the treasure was likely a fiction. And she didn't even know where to start with expressing an interest in it. Besides, was it stealing a march on the very kind gentlemen who were actually pursuing it, including the exceedingly thoughtful Viscount Severn? And how did it connect with the papers she had seen in Lady Evangeline's possession? Was the lady pursuing the treasure too? If that were the case, then it could be considered part of Dria's responsibilities. On the other hand, if she were hunting the treasure as a part of her employment, it wasn't likely she would gain much benefit from finding it.

Of course, she wouldn't. She never gained.

All she ever got was pin money while the rest of her wages were sent to her family. That was the arrangement that had been set up when she was a girl, and it had continued with her transfer to Esther Bastion's company. At least that change had resulted in the pin money. When she had been a girl, she hadn't even had that. But neither had Mary, really, so neither of them had given the matter thought.

Now she thought on it with great vigor, even as she accompanied Lady Evangeline to inspect the work being done on her house on Spring Street.

That had been a lovely excursion. What a handsome house. It wasn't nearly as large or grand as Everleigh House, nor, from what Eve told her, anything on a scale like the house she had lived in with her late husband, but that was part of its appeal to the wealthy woman, from what Adriana could tell.

No one really needed such a large house unless they were going to be entertaining foreign dignitaries or royalty. Even the Earl of Everleigh seemed to be hardly highly enough placed within Society to need so much space. But with five sons and their families, it was likely very useful, and with all the additional family members some of the Northcotts seemed inclined to collect, including herself, the large number of rooms clearly were advantageous.

But Lady Evangeline didn't require nearly so much, and she seemed quite delighted with the new house her late husband had bought for her prior to his sudden death. Mr. Smythe was clearly pleased as well, although Adriana heard him grumbling about staying in England forever. She hadn't understood the meaning of his words but they had prompted light laughter from his fiancée, so Adriana assumed it was some sort of inside joke between the two of them.

The workmen had just finished with the wall hangings and the entire house had an odorous scent of glue and paint that Adriana suspected couldn't be quite healthful. Lady Evangeline evidently agreed.

"We can't move in just yet, I'm afraid. Not with this stench filling the place. Oh bother. I hadn't thought of that result when I ordered it all done at once. I thought it would be more convenient to move in and not have to live amongst the dirt and dust of going room by room."

"You were quite correct in that assumption. And if we went room by room, we would only drag out the stink, don't you think?" Sean pointed out in a cheerfully reasonable tone.

"But I did wish to get settled."

"We'll just have to do it together then. We'll have all the windows opened and air the place out. Surely it shouldn't take more than a few days for the smell to settle and move on, don't you suppose?" Dria was surprised when he turned to her. "Have you any experience with such things?"

"I'm afraid I don't." She stumbled out the words. "But we might be able to ask Lord Severn."

"Oh yes, the chemist should know when it would be safe to move in. Then we'll arrange for our vows, and we'll move in together." Sean turned to his bride-to-be with a wide, delighted grin that felt like a stab to Dria's belly. It was unusual for her to feel jealousy, but she was fairly certain that was what was behind the unfamiliar pang. She had to work hard not to sigh over it.

"That is probably better than my moving in alone," Evangeline agreed immediately before turning to Dria. "Well, I wouldn't have been alone," she added before turning back to Sean. "But if it's to be our home together, then you're right, we should move here at the same time."

Adriana felt as though she were eavesdropping on a conversation she shouldn't be privy to and wished herself elsewhere. Her feelings must have been written on her face because suddenly Lady Evangeline laughed and put her hand through Dria's bent elbow.

"You are being the best sport about all of this, my dear Adriana. I know it must be challenging for you to take on all these new tasks. But I must say, you are taking to the work quite admirably. It would seem there is a businesswoman underneath the prim and proper lady after all."

Dria almost cringed at the other woman's words but managed to keep her reaction within bounds by the exertion of her will. She might be sufficiently intelligent to learn what was required, but she wasn't going to give up on doing what she herself thought was proper.

Not that she could say there was anything overtly improper about anything Evangeline had thus far shown her about conducting business. Yes, it seemed likely they would need to expose themselves to rougher company than she was used to, but the same could be said depending where one went to purchase household supplies, if that were within one's responsibilities. Dria was aware that some ladies liked to make such purchases themselves, as it helped them control the budget more closely. In all actuality, Evangeline's activities were only extreme in scale, not really any different from the activities of a busy housewife.

When looked at from that perspective, there was nothing for Adriana to be concerned about.

Except maintaining her charge's reputation until she was safely wed. If the calf's eyes these two were making at each other was any indication, it would be best if that date was sped along.

"Have you been to see the bishop yet?" she asked Sean, suddenly prompting laughter from both him and Lady Evangeline.

"Are we giving you a toothache with our lovesick ways? Poor Adriana. Again, you are holding up well."

Evangeline laughed and shook her head. “We haven’t yet decided if we want to go with a special license or have the banns read. What would you do if you were in my place? You are likely far more experienced in Society matters than either of us.”

“I couldn’t begin to form an opinion, my lady,” Adriana started stiffly.

“I find that difficult to believe. Everyone forms their opinions left, right, and center. You just don’t know if you want to share it,” Evangeline said with amusement clear in her voice.

“What are the pros and cons you are weighing?” Adriana asked, trying to be brave and give her employer what she asked for.

“Despite Sean’s slowly evolving opinions about the English, I don’t wish to be ruined socially. I would like to have the option to remain at least a little active in Society or to be received if I wish to do so. In view of that, I don’t want to do anything that would be considered scandalous. So, would it be better to take the time, read the banns, wait the few weeks, and then have whatever sort of ceremony we’d like? Or should we just go ahead and wed and get on with our lives?”

“What makes you think anyone would object to your marrying without waiting?”

“Haste smacks of necessity. I would hate to have anyone counting the days were we to be blessed with a child from our marriage, for one thing. For another, I would never want anyone to think we hadn’t waited due to any other low-class reason, especially considering Sean’s status due to his wretch of a father.”

“I don’t want to make a splash at St. George’s or anything like that, but I don’t want to appear like we have anything to hide, either,” Sean added.

Adriana nodded in sympathy. “I can see that it would be difficult to choose. And then there’s your businesses and even this house," she added with a sigh. "Could you bear it, and even would Roderick and Lucy mind, if you were to stay with them for the three weeks and maybe wed at Everleigh House? Lucy mentioned some more of the Northcotts were planning to come to Town. That would surely lend legitimacy to the proceedings. And even though you're anxious to get on with your lives together, surely three weeks will fly by with wings."

"You speak wisely, my dear," Evangeline answered. "I am inclined to agree with you even though I quite hate the thought of waiting in some ways. But perhaps we could make it a little splash. Wed privately but then get Everleigh to host a ball afterward. We could even include your Miss Bastion, if she and his lordship would ever finalize their plans."

"Oh, no, you needn't worry yourself about them."

"Don't you think Esther would like it?"

"She would love it beyond anything, I'm sure. But do you want to share your special occasion like that?" Dria was skeptical.

"I would really rather not have any extra attention, at all, to be perfectly truthful. I just want to do what will lend us the greatest possibility of success."

"If you truly wouldn't mind sharing, then I would think you've come across the ideal suggestion. While she isn't truly High Society, Miss Bastion is perfectly acceptable, and Lord Phillips is a viscount who has been accepted everywhere. I don't feel that I've truly come to know him very deeply in that I cannot say why he hasn't yet wed her, but I do think they would both be happy to share a special evening with you, especially if it were to be held at Everleigh House. It might be more of a splash as you said than either of you are in favor of, but it will certainly be well supported by even the highest sticklers of the *ton*, especially if the earl and his heir were convinced to attend."

"Isn't Society the silliest?" Lady Evangeline asked with little rancor.

"I certainly cannot argue with that sentiment," Dria returned mildly, prompting laughter from Sean, followed by grumbling about the daft English.

"Very well, then, let us return to the others and start things in motion. How fortuitous for us that it's nearly Sunday," Sean said, adding, "I shan't wait a day longer than necessary. Let us say on the third Monday from now?"

Dria laughed along with the others, but she couldn't have truly said what motivated it. Was she happy that she had a position for at least three more weeks? Or was she truly happy for the people in her life? It would seem all the people would be changing before the month was out, and that put cold dread into the pit of her stomach. But she wasn't about to cry craven over it. Esther had promised to make certain she was cared for. So had Evangeline, for that matter. She shouldn't let her worries distract her from the tasks that were before her. It was quite likely they were about to launch into complex plans for two very different weddings.

In terms of rapid planning, it would seem favour was on their side as Lord Phillips had finally called upon Esther, or so they found when they arrived back at Everleigh House. Lady Evangeline was able to present the idea to everyone at once. At least everyone involved in the decision making.

"Oh, what a delightful idea," Lucy said immediately. "I know all my sisters will wish to participate in launching you both into your wedded bliss," she added with a wide smile and twinkling eyes.

Adriana found their hostess charming and could understand why Roderick was smitten with her, but she could also tell the more fastidious Lord Philips was uncomfortable with the display of delight. It added to her concern for Esther's future, and she wondered if she ought to broach the subject with her friend. But were they friends? Dria had been Esther's companion for years, oh heavens, six years now. But were they really friends? They had each always kept a slight wall between them. Dria had always welcomed that reserve after her experience with Mary, but now, witnessing the scholars and their family-like friendship, she realized she had missed out on something precious by that very reserve. She would try to talk to Esther about her future happiness, she resolved. The employment was about to end, there wasn't anything for her to lose. And she did care for the other woman.

The rest of the afternoon, before they had to ready themselves for supper, was spent in making their plans. Adriana's hand nearly cramped from all the notes she had to take, keeping track of what each woman wanted, since there were two weddings to plan. It was agreed that Esther and Lord Philips would marry three days before the ball while Evangeline and Sean would wed the morning of the ball. Esther and Adriana had already spoken with the vicar at St. George's and knew it was available that day, as she had been dithering about dates for a couple of weeks. That was one more note Dria made, she needed to reconfirm that the date was still available, since they had spoken to them a few days ago. It was entirely possible, considering one of the purposes of the Season was to arrange marriages, some other hopeful couple had spoken for the date.

"You could have your wedding breakfast here, if you'd like," Lucy said with a charming smile aimed at Esther. "Or you could just wait for the ball, whatever you would like."

"Or we could host a breakfast at our own home," Lord Philips finally spoke up. "Do you think that might be best?"

Esther stared at her betrothed, clearly stunned by the offer. "But I haven't even met your servants yet," she blurted before embarrassment flooded her features. She hadn't intended to admit as much in front of the others.

"That can easily be rectified," Lord Philips returned.

"It isn't usual for the bride and groom to host," Lucy said gently but then added, "Of course, you might start a new fashion."

Esther looked wildly at Adriana as though seeking assistance. Dria couldn't imagine what was best for the woman. "Perhaps it would be easier and more relaxing to have something smaller here at Everleigh House immediately after the ceremony, just a luncheon with the household and a few friends and family members. Then the ball the evening of Eve and Sean's wedding for the four of you, and then the new Lady Philips could plan her own grander entertainment a couple weeks afterward. A dinner, a musicale, or a smaller ball. I haven't seen your townhouse, my lord, so I'm not sure if you have a ballroom, but we could arrange for something that will still be within the season of your wedding."

"Oh, I do like that idea, Adriana, to make it a season of festivities rather than just one day. Thank you." The smile she extended toward Adriana was filled with gratitude that seemed out of proportion to what she had done, but there was naught Dria could do to assure the woman that no thanks were necessary. She was only worried about her employer's fiancé's reaction. His stoic expression revealed very little of his thoughts.

"I agree," Lucy added. "And the other Northcott women will still be about, so we could all lend a hand in whatever way you'd like."

"Thank you," Lord Philips replied in a stiff tone without really making a commitment. Dria was uncomfortable, but Esther didn't appear to notice or mind. He soon took his leave, and everyone else dispersed to make their preparations for the evening.

"We will have to return to St. George's to ensure they still have availability that day," Adriana said to Esther as she watched the maid finishing up the other woman's hairstyle.

"Oh, yes, thank you for remembering that, Adriana," Esther replied, not appearing concerned in the least.

"Do you think his lordship is pleased with the development?" Dria sked, hesitant to stir up trouble.

"Oh, I should think so. He wasn't in a great rush to begin with, but he does want to have everything wrapped up before the current Parliament ends its sessions so he can bring me with him back to his estate."

"Don't you mind that you haven't seen his home or met any of his servants? How will you know how to go on?"

Esther sighed and turned to face Adriana. "I don't think it's so unusual that a bride hasn't met the servants. But I don't know how I'll go on without you to help me. I am starting to think marriage might be very strange."

Adriana laughed. "You're only starting to think that?"

Esther laughed along in good spirits before sobering and leveling a surprisingly searching gaze upon Dria. "What about you? This development, while good for me, seems to lend itself to your being without employment within three weeks. Are you desperately disappointed?"

"Disappointed isn't the right word, and I already realized it was likely to coincide at least somewhat, but I will admit to being a trifle anxious on the matter." She took a breath that she released gently. "One point of comfort, though, is that Evangeline has mentioned she might like to keep me on as an assistant even if she no longer needs a companion, since she has found me to be a quick study in her affairs. But in addition to that, Viscount Severn has mentioned that his cousins, his uncle's daughters, might be in need of my services. I also wrote to Mary and her former guardians. So, I might have a different issue of more employment than I require."

"Kind of like right now," Esther pointed out with a raised eyebrow.

"Exactly," Adriana nodded with a puff of laughter.

"I still think you ought to consider marriage." Esther held up her hand when it was obvious Adriana was going to argue. "I know, you don't agree, and you are concerned for your family. But I still argue your family ought to have found their own way by now, and you need to look to your own future." She sighed and shook her head. "I know you want to find another position and I promised you I'd help, and I will. But I still think marriage would be a more secure future for you. What of these inventors and scientists? One of them could make a fine match if he were to discover something lucrative. You could support your family and still have a future for yourself."

Adriana smiled, a little sad at the thought. "I know you mean well, Esther, but do you think I ought to enter into a marriage with all the dependents I have? Who would want to take all that on?"

"A rich man would barely notice."

"But none of the gentlemen you're thinking of are rich, at least not yet."

Esther frowned. Adriana didn't want her worrying about her personal affairs, at least not yet. The other woman had never had to be concerned about money ever in her life. She couldn't understand the situation fully. Adriana didn't blame her for that. It wasn't her problem.

"Do you think you'll be happy with Lord Philips? Aren't you concerned about ending up in the countryside far from all that's familiar to you?"

Esther's gaze turned away as though she were searching the middle distance. "I do think I'll be happy with him. I know it isn't going to be the grand love affair that either the Northcotts nor your Lady Evangeline and her mathematician seem to be enjoying. At least not from the beginning. But I am ready to make a change. I've realized that I want a more settled existence and I quite like the thought of bearing a title."

Adriana laughed a little. "That sounds a little mercenary, doesn't it?"

"Perhaps. I will be paying for it, after all. But I am going in with clear eyes, and I trust the gentleman will treat me respectfully at the very least. And I am beginning to think that children will be delightful."

Adriana wasn't sure if the other woman was looking high enough, but it wasn't her life to live. "I pray for your happiness."

"I know you do. I am content. This is what I want," she said seriously before her smile widened. "And I'm thrilled at the arrangements. Will you be free to come with me in the morning to check on St. George's?"

"Absolutely," Adriana vowed even though she wasn't certain. She would make it work. Somehow.

The rest of the evening went by in a blur of fashionable activity.

Chapter Sixteen

Ellis was surprised to find the house abustle with activity when he returned to Town.

"Are you coming to the ball or the rout?"

"You must hurry and change."

"Supper is in ten minutes."

This from various sides as he entered the room the gentlemen shared. The others were already dressed for the evening.

"I hadn't thought to go out tonight," he said. "I've been riding all day."

"You aren't in your dotage, man. Hurry and clean up and join us. We'll be surrounded by potions and books soon enough. This is only days out of time."

"I heard the Northcotts are staying for at least a month now, on account of the weddings," one of the gentlemen spoke up, eliciting groans from the others.

"A month? What about my work?"

"Forget work, what about the treasure?"

"Well, that gives us a month to find the treasure, then, if we don't return to the estate in the meantime."

Ellis snorted lightly but didn't bother telling the fellows he thought their talk of treasure was ridiculous. It wasn't for him to criticize their pursuits. He needed to focus on his own, already established, issues and responsibilities. Now that he had agreed, or promised or however you wanted to word it, to help his cousins, that needed to be a priority for him. And with that in mind, he needed to assure himself of a dependable income. Sure, a treasure trove would be wonderful and quite helpful under the circumstances, but a dream wouldn't keep coal in the burner or food on the table if he didn't get his extraction process finalized and sold. Or he could figure out some other use for his chemical knowledge, he supposed. But he needed to know now or very soon that he had dependable income. Steady, dependable income. And a plan for the girls.

He couldn't go haring off after treasures. Some of the fellows were still the dreamy students they had always been. He wasn't so sure he had ever been like that, even though he had loved everything about learning.

Knowing he was Viscount Severn from a young age had made his circumstances vastly different than some of the others. And then coming to understand that his position as Severn was actually not well established had altered things further for him. Now he was even more determined to ensure he had himself set up for independence. It was the only way he would be able to help his cousins, even if he were replaced as the heir. If they were to gain a baby brother, the boy wouldn't be able to do much for his sisters for at least twenty years. By then, all of them should be well settled and with families of their own.

Which he, too, would like for himself.

That made him think of the delectable but oh so serious Miss Adriana Adams. In some ways she was the perfect wife for the simple Mr. Ellis Dorval. But not so much for the future Earl of Beaverbrook. Ellis shook his head. He was in difficult circumstances. So was Adriana. She hadn't indicated any marked interest in him. He ought not think of it.

But he had an evening to get through. He followed the other scholars' advice and hurried to change into clothes that weren't mud spattered from a ride across fields that afternoon.

"How was your day?"

The soft, gentle voice was a surprise, coming from behind his left elbow where he leaned against a door jamb at the Lady Yorkleigh rout later that evening.

"Good evening to you, too," Ellis said, turning with a smile to greet Adriana, surprised that she had approached him. She had been so quiet during supper. "My day was quite enjoyable, thank you for asking. You were nearly completely mute at supper. I assumed your day wasn't nearly as delightful as mine."

"I was resting," she answered with a smile.

His eyebrows lifted toward his hairline. "At the supper table, in a crowd?"

She laughed lightly but nodded eagerly. "It is something I learned to do years ago. When you are always at someone's beck and call, there is never time for a nap or a true rest. I have learned to empty my thoughts and take a needed break whenever I can be assured that my employer will be looked after. Like, as you said, at a crowded supper table. Even though I couldn't truly sleep, just being able to rest my thoughts for a moment is sufficient at times like these. I also find looking at a country scene either real or painted does nearly as well for me."

"That is quite remarkable," Ellis said mildly. "The fellows who study psychology at Cambridge or Oxford would likely love to examine you."

She laughed again but shook her head. "I don't think there's anything study-worthy about it. I'm certain it works the same for everyone only no one bothers to try it as their circumstances are different."

Ellis shook his head as well but turned the subject. "What made your day such that you needed to rest during supper?"

Again, she smiled gently. "Both of our brides-to-be have chosen their wedding dates and how they will be celebrated. And they will essentially overlap and coincide. So much planning is about to ensue or has started already, in reality. Thankfully, most of Miss Bastion's arrangements have already been decided upon, we just need to confirm the date is available, and all will be in order. And Lucy has eagerly taken on much of the arrangements or really all of them as pertains to Everleigh House, which includes a luncheon for Esther and Lord Philips and a ball for both couples a few days later."

"Much has changed in a few hours, then."

Adriana nodded but her smile didn't quite reach her eyes. Ellis' concern for her notched higher. "You are worrying, aren't you?"

Her small laugh sounded a little more hysterical than usual, but she lifted a shoulder as though to dismiss his question. "I wouldn't say my worry is any more than usual, to be honest. In fact, knowing the date has taken away a little of the worry, since the uncertainty is lessened. Now I know when things will change again. And for certain, Miss Bastion shan't need me three weeks from now, but it is possible Evangeline shall keep me, and that will be easier than the current situation. Or something else will present itself." She paused for a second, nodding. "Of course, I don't love any sort of uncertainty. Not knowing exactly what will happen after three weeks from now doesn't lift my heart. But such is life. I shall manage."

"I spoke with my cousins on the subject of you, as a matter of fact."

"Oh, how kind of you. I enjoyed your tales at supper of your visit with them. They sound delightfully active."

"I didn't think you had heard."

She laughed a little, again, this time sounding more joyful with it. "I can rest and listen at the same time. I am a woman of many talents." She waved her hand as though to dismiss the jest and asked about his visit. "How are you feeling after seeing them? Was it truly the first time you had gone specifically to see the girls?"

"Yes, it was, and the household reaction was just what you would expect. The servants were shocked and didn't know what to do with me as I had never just dropped by unannounced before. The butler kept repeating that his lordship was in Town and surely I must be mistaken." Ellis chuckled, watching her eyes widen. "Once I had convinced them that I was, in fact, there to see the girls, then they didn't know where to make that happen. Finally, my oldest cousin was summoned, and she agreed that the nursery was the best place for me despite the blow to my dignity."

Her eyes warmed as though she didn't agree with his sarcastic assessment. "And how long has it been since you've seen the inside of a nursery?"

"At least twenty years, I would think," Ellis replied. "My dignity did remain intact, though. Even the very youngest of the girls managed to keep their spills contained to themselves, and my valet wasn't made to retire with a cold compress at the sight of me. Except perhaps my boots. I rode and it was muckier than I expected, so the servants were displeased over my state when I returned."

"To be sure," Adriana replied with a twinkle in her eyes. "But that tells me nothing of the girls. Were they all atwitter with your arrival?"

"Somewhat, except Seraphina, the second oldest. She acted as though I had inconvenienced the lot of them. And likely I had. I interrupted their usual routine and I'm sure the youngest, especially, were difficult to contain after the sugar they partook of and the stimulation from the excitement of a visitation in the schoolroom." Ellis sighed and shook his head again, leaning in closer to her so she could hear him over the sound of the milling fellow guests and yet not to be overheard. "To be fair, I hadn't given the matter the least bit of thought. I decided I wished to speak with them, so I went. That was poorly done of me, wasn't it?"

Now her gaze was filled with admiration and sympathy and Ellis felt his chest begin to puff up unnaturally.

"As you have admitted, you have almost no experience with children aside from when you were one yourself. Your intentions were pure. And I'm sure the sisters and the servants ensured the youngest children didn't have anything that would harm them. Of course, there would be excess excitement brought on by your presence, but that would happen whether you had warned them or not, don't you think?"

"I suppose that's true."

"Did the older girls have any thoughts about their future? Did they appreciate your offer to assist them? Or perhaps you found that it was all much more in hand than you had thought?"

Ellis sighed. "No, I was right, unfortunately. My uncle has been far too occupied with his quest for a son to consider his daughters or their future. The oldest two really ought to have debuted already, or very soon. Well, perhaps not Sera, not already, but Cordelia, for certain ought to have already launched. They don't have any expectations of it actually happening, though, despite my offer to assist. But they did admit that if my uncle agreed, they would be pleased to come up for a Season. I mentioned you to them, and they were also pleased at the prospect of your company, but again, contingent on Beaverbrook's agreement. I also told them the Northcotts would likely help, but I haven't actually spoken to Lucy about it yet."

Now Adriana's warm, generous smile widened further, and her tinkle of laughter filled his chest. "You know she will be thrilled at the prospect provided the timing of her confinement allows it. But knowing Lucy, she will volunteer any manner of family members and friends into the situation, so you needn't be concerned. I heard about how all your scholarly friends called their family and friends up to scratch to support Evangeline and Sean. I am certain you could call upon your connections in a similar manner."

"Perhaps, but an entire Season is far different from one ball."

"True, but if you find the right matron, one who is perhaps a little bored and without her own obligations, you should be set."

"Or a well-situated companion?"

Ellis appreciated that she didn't deny him outright, but she did laugh a little ruefully. "I'm not sure I'm well-enough situated to be able to sponsor anyone's debut, Severn. Chaperone, escort, accompany, those are my strengths, and I will happily do those for your cousins if they'll have me when I'm through here. But we will have to call upon others for assistance to properly launch them." Her gaze then turned speculative. "Of course, you could always marry someone who could properly launch them. That would solve the problem nicely. I am reasonably sure Viscountess Severn would be all the rage."

"I'm not certain launching my cousins is the proper reason for my marrying," Ellis began.

"Why not?" she asked, clearly jesting with him if the twinkle in her eyes was any indication. He found her deeply enticing in a funning mood. He had to remind himself that he wasn't ready to pursue any sort of dalliance. But she had more to say. "Didn't you say there are seven girls? Your wife would be kept quite busy for years to come. And then it would be time to launch your own brood. Surely you ought to be getting on with that responsibility before too long."

"Now you are starting to sound like Beaverbrook."

She laughed anew, sounding far more light-hearted than she had when he'd first seen her that evening. "Speaking of Beaverbrook, why has he not launched his own offspring? It does seem a trifle irregular that you are seeing to it."

Worry now gripped him. "But not irregular enough to cause a problem, would you say?"

She quickly sobered and put out a hand to his arm as though to offer comfort. "It needn't, as long as he cooperates. It is likely everyone already considers him eccentric."

"That is very true," he agreed with her, heaving a sigh of relief. "So, you will do it? If Beaverbrook agrees? You'll join my cousins and chaperone them for however long they need you?"

She started to nod but then a frown creased her forehead. "Do they not have governesses or companions already? I know you didn't think so when we discussed it earlier, but you were just there, was it not mentioned?"

"They do have a governess, only one for seven girls. Most of the girls are still essentially in the schoolroom, at least five of them. I would say one governess for all seven isn't nearly enough."

"Goodness, no, I wouldn't think so, either. Well, then, absolutely, yes, if your uncle will agree to my hiring, I would be happy to accompany your cousins. I will do my best to escort them for their debut as well, but there are things they likely need to do to prepare, as well. I wonder if we ought to discuss those with your uncle at the same time. In a certain way, it is multiple issues." She startled as the music drew to a close. "And this isn't really the time or place to discuss any of this, is it?" she asked with a little laugh. "Perhaps over breakfast?" she added with a question mark clearly evident in her tone even as she blushed. It was a trifle odd to be discussing breakfast with a woman who was not a member of his family.

With a nod and a wave, she left his side as abruptly as she had joined him. Ellis hoped his conflicting feelings weren't written upon his features as he watched her go.

Chapter Seventeen

Adriana wanted to die. Or rather she suspected she was going to choke to death on the mortification that threatened to suffocate her. How had she lost all sense and stood about conversing with a viscount for what was surely at least fifteen minutes? It was not done. Not by her at any rate. There was sure to be gossip. Or maybe not. No one would think Viscount Severn was courting her. It was more likely there would be words bandied about her setting her cap at the gentleman. How perfectly lowering. And not at all the thing to raise her position in regard to his cousins. If it were thought that she was dallying with the viscount, her presence in his cousins' lives was only going to cause them trouble rather than help them.

Take a breath, Dria, she admonished herself as she spiraled into panic.

No one was going to think she was dallying with the viscount. It wasn't likely anyone had even noticed they had been talking and, even if they had been noticed, there had been nothing untoward about the conversation. Just because she found him attractive and appealing didn't mean anything. This was not her future. She was not a marriage-minded debutante nor a widow or matron. She was a companion. Nearly invisible. And certainly not a participant in the Marriage Mart.

And saying they could discuss it over breakfast was not a salacious thing to say. Surely not.

Adriana addressed the comment that had mortified her the most, at least in her own mind. It had sounded scandalous when she'd said it. But surely it wasn't, was it? It was practical. They were staying in the same dwelling. An extremely large dwelling. The breakfast room was a public space in that very large dwelling. There was nothing salacious or scandalous or particularly interesting about their meeting for a conversation there. It was entirely likely there would be others present. It was all perfectly innocent.

Then why didn't it feel that way?

Why were butterflies clogging up her inner workings?

Why did she feel like it was lovely and private and intimate and all sorts of other ridiculous sensations?

Because she was an idiot. It wasn't any of those things. It was a practical meeting in which to discuss how she could help his cousins and thus ensure her employment for another decade or so. Or perhaps just another year since surely if one sister wed, she would take on the rest of them. But Dria didn't want to get ahead of herself.

Beaverbrook might not agree.

Especially not if he thought she had set her cap at his heir.

Taking a deep breath in through her nose and blowing it slowly out of her mouth, Adriana managed to still her racing thoughts even as she looked around for her two charges. In the end, Evangeline and Sean decided to join them at the rout rather than the ball the others were going to. Dria needed to ensure both her couples were sufficiently chaperoned as well as supplied with whatever they needed to enjoy their evenings.

There wasn't time for her to dally nor to have a breakdown after said non-dalliance. After another restorative deep breath, suddenly Dria's life was a blur and the next three weeks passed before she could even blink. In later weeks, months, or even years, she didn't think she would ever be able to recount what had happened during that strange period when the flow of time seemed different for her than for others. Except maybe when it came to the treasure hunt, but that was a fantasy that only kept her thoughts warm in the approximately thirty seconds that passed between when her head hit the pillow and she was fast asleep.

But it was now the wedding day.

Well, Lady Evangeline and Mr. Sean Smythe's wedding day. Wedding day number two to be exact. Wedding number one, that of Miss Esther Bastion and Lord Philips, Viscount Droitmuir, had taken place in a dramatic, decadent swirl at St. George's three days prior, followed by an abundant and delicious meal for the residents of Everleigh House, whose numbers had swelled considerably, and a few friends and family members invited by the viscount. It had been nearly a crush and Esther had been gratified. So had Lucy, much to the household's amusement.

After Dria had waved off the bride and groom from the top of the stairs of Everleigh House, she hadn't seen them since. It was strange after more than six years of being together with Esther for nearly every waking moment, but that was likely as it should be. Dria never would have thought she would miss the exacting and rather cool woman, but they had grown closer in the passing years than she had realized. Adriana was looking forward to seeing the newlyweds that day, if only to see how the bride went on. Considering it hadn't been a love match and Dria feared the viscount had wed Esther for her deep pockets, she wanted to ensure the woman remained content with her decision.

Now wasn't the time to be dithering in anxious thoughts, though. She had a lengthy list of things she needed to attend to in order for Eve and Sean to have a special day. Dria was well aware the young noblewoman was anxious about the day and not looking forward to the ball that evening. With how disappointing she had found her first marriage, it was understandable Evangeline was struggling with nerves at the last minute before wedding a second time, despite how much she loved the gentleman in question. Adding in a large, High Society social event on top of everything only made for it to be a trial for everyone.

Well, perhaps not Lucy Northcott. That woman seemed to thrive on the strangest things. She was fluttering about the house getting herself involved in every aspect of every plan despite her husband following after her trying to keep her from overextending herself in her delicate condition.

But despite her diminutive size and the fact that she was with child, Adriana didn't really consider there to be anything delicate about Lucy Northcott. The woman could be a tyrant if she thought someone was interfering with her intentions. And it would seem she intended to marry off every single woman who had been, well, single at the same time as she had been. Dria often wondered if that included her but thus far, she was fairly certain she had managed to escape the young matron's matchmaking intentions. She was afraid it might only be a matter of time unless Roderick could convince his wife to return to their estate.

"You made it."

Ugh! Could she sound any more breathy and stupid? And what did it matter if he made it? Viscount Severn was nothing to her. A mere acquaintance. No one who should make her heart lift and jump about like it was trying to hop right out of her chest. Perhaps it was merely the anxiety she had been experiencing in connection with the weddings and her changing circumstances.

Or maybe it was the warmth in his gaze as he looked intently into her eyes.

"I made it," he agreed, his low deep voice doing inexplicable things to her midsection. "Are you well? I never meant to be gone all this time, but there has been much to occupy me." He said it in a warm, familiar tone as though he needed to explain himself to her.

She tried to dismiss it. "I heard your business was concluded quite nicely. Roderick was crowing about it at the supper table this week despite Lucy's hushing."

"It was a complete success, I'm very happy to report. I cannot wait to show it to you."

Adriana blinked. Wouldn't that be lovely? But how was she to witness his extraction process and see his success? She was a mere paid companion. If she reminded herself often enough, she might be able to convince her heart to stop being ridiculous. If only she had found a treasure. Then she could be like Eve or Esther and plot her own course in life.

But she wasn't. She was the rather dull and obscure Miss Adriana Adams, no one of any particular note. The treasure was just a fantasy that would never come true. But it had been an enjoyable thought that had helped her survive the chaos of these weeks.

Now things would return to a modicum of calm and she could get on with the sensible side of life.

Well, perhaps tomorrow she would. Today was a precious whirl that was going to turn her head almost completely. The moment of Sean and Eve's exchange of vows was the most romantic moment Dria had ever witnessed.

Adriana hadn't thought she was the least bit romantically inclined and determined she was far too preoccupied with the practicalities of the day to even really pay much attention to the private proceedings in the large withdrawing room.

That contradictory thought brought her amusement that stemmed the flow of her tears, much to her relief. It was a private moment only in that it wasn't in a large church with anyone from the public able to attend. No, rather, it was merely all the residents of Everleigh House crowded into the room. It wasn't a crush, but it also wasn't only the bride and groom and a member of the clergy as Eve had hoped. And yet as the bride and groom exchanged their words in hushed, reverent tones, Dria felt as though the audience were eavesdropping on a very intimate moment for the newlywed couple.

It would seem everyone else had felt similarly as there was a hush that fell over the group and barely a whisper could be heard in the large room as the minister pronounced them husband and wife. Then Sean let out a whoop of joy, and his scholarly friends shouted along with him in a less than scholarly manner that seemed to amuse rather than offend the High Society guests. Even the bride's stodgy brother could be seen with an indulgent smile upon his rather pinched features.

Thinking about the wedding that morning was the last almost peaceful thought Adriana was able to enjoy for the rest of the evening as she found herself running from pillar to post throughout the entire house keeping everything arranged exactly as it had been planned. She was relieved to note that Mr. Roderick Northcott had taken his wife in hand and was keeping her from running herself ragged. Worrying about Lucy was the last thing Dria could handle that day. If the young matron were to harm her little one inadvertently with her determination to see to everything for her friends, Adriana wouldn't have been able to forgive herself. But she should have known the gentleman would be keeping a close eye on his wife.

Before Roderick was able to insist his wife leave off her activities, though, Lucy had whisked the guests off to the large dining room for a delicious meal of fresh, hot rolls, ham and other meats, as well as the eggs that were mysteriously kept warm. Then most of the household dispersed. The bride and groom went off to inspect their home on Spring Street as they now were co-owners and about to become cohabitants.

Adriana had wished to accompany them if only to ensure Sean didn't do something to worry his new bride. Dria was well aware the young lady was concerned about all her newfound wealth and the rights her husband would have once they wed. Adriana was almost completely certain Mr. Smythe wasn't at all mercenary in his desire to wed with Evangeline, but it was possible he could still say something stupid to upset his new wife.

But of course, it wasn't her place to attend to the bride this day. She wasn't even going to remain the woman's companion, as Sean had agreed that clerks would suffice to assist them both. Adriana had nearly finalized the arrangements to become companion to Lord Beaverbrook's daughters. That position had seemed nearly impossible to fill. Dria still wasn't sure how Severn had arranged it. She had been certain Lord Beaverbrook would refuse the suggestion outright since he seemed so preoccupied with pursuing his efforts at producing an heir to displace his nephew.

But Ellis had persisted as he had promised his cousins and Adriana herself.

Adriana shook her head. Now wasn't the time to be dwelling on any of this. With the wedding breakfast over and Lucy tucked up in bed for a nap, she needed to see to the rest of the arrangements for the ball.

The rest of the day, evening, and night passed in a blur. It felt to Adriana as though time wasn't working properly. For the most part, it flew by as though the sun or the earth or whatever Pierce Darby the astronomer had said when attempting to explain to her about how time worked. But it felt that it was moving much too quickly for her to keep up with all the arrangements that had been planned. Thankfully the Northcott and Everleigh servants were impeccably trained, and Dria didn't have to worry overmuch. Of course, she was an excellent worrier and found herself flitting from task to task checking to ensure all was well only to find that it was getting on quite well without her.

She would have felt completely unnecessary except that even when she found the servants doing exactly as they ought, there were questions to be answered and directions to give. It was reassuring to her. And her need to be needed felt well and truly assuaged that day.

But then Ellis stopped her and asked her to the dance floor and for the five or ten or however many minutes the waltz took, time was no longer running at even its usual pace. It nearly felt as though it were standing still. Even the unscholarly Adriana Adams knew that wasn't possible but fancifully she thought it and didn't even care. She was happy for it to slow down for it meant she could savour the experience, squeezing every last drop of enjoyment from it for surely, she wouldn't get to do so again.

What a relief Miss Bastion, or rather Lady Droitmuir, had insisted she learn the waltz at the same time as she did. Unfortunately, Esther had made Adriana learn the male role so they could practice together. A fact that led Ellis to much amusement as he huskily whispered into her ear.

"I know you're highly capable but you really must allow me to lead us."

A part of Adriana wanted to fall through the floor and die a thousand deaths of mortification but the rest of her shivered with delight over the entire experience. Not least of which was the tickle of his warm breath on the shell of her ear.

It seemed to her that the orchestra had found the longest waltz ever written, but Adriana couldn't be bothered to mind. She ought to have told them they should stick to the usual length of dances and perhaps she would do so when Ellis brought her back to the side lines but for now, she would concentrate on cataloguing every last sensation.

She couldn't even decide which was her favourite.

Was it the heat that seemed to radiate between them as the dance brought them nearly scandalously close? It wasn't the most rigorous dance ever thought up, but it was far from sedate either. Between the exertion required and the flush that seemed to always spread through her in the viscount's presence, Adriana felt as though she might melt.

Of course, that could be attributed to the firm clasp of the viscount's gentle grip. That sensation seemed to be rather contradictory. Was it firm or was it gentle? Somehow it was both. Adriana felt as though she would be safe in the gentleman's arms if ever she needed to be. Of course, that was the most foolish thought to have presented itself to her mind yet. She couldn't possibly be safe in a man's arms. That was the way to ruin, and then where would she be?

Adriana refused to think about her future during the dance, so she returned to enumerating the delicious feelings she was experiencing.

Ellis didn't trouble her with too much conversation. Not to say that she ever minded conversing with the man. But it seemed to Dria that he was just as content as she was to merely enjoy the experience in the moment.

But he did on occasion utter an observation or ask a question.

"You are remarkably skilled at the dance, now that you are no longer trying to direct my steps."

His teasing voice could be felt in her chest and in her ear. She almost shivered but managed to neither do something so foolish nor miss a step despite the distraction his words provided.

She nodded her head with what she feared was a dreamy smile as she acknowledged his words without a comment of her own. What was she to say to that? Argue the point? She had no desire to do so. She was flattered beyond measure that he would say so. She had almost no practice at following a gentleman's lead, only from the one lesson Esther had paid for. After that, they had muddled through, practicing on their own.

"You have done well in planning this event. You've likely been inundated with everyone telling you this, but I thought I ought to mention it despite being part of the chorus."

This time she really did almost miss her step as she struggled to control the surge of emotion his words caused.

"Why that is quite the loveliest thing anyone has said to me in an age," she said, trying not to allow herself to give full rein to her feelings.

"But surely everyone has been telling you the same all day," Ellis exclaimed even as she shook her head and tried very hard not to step closer into the dance.

"No, I'm afraid no one has seemed to notice that I had anything to do with any part of today. Of course, the brides have been appreciative, but they are remarkably distracted," she added with a smile to dissipate the sound of complaint from her words.

"But it would seem you've done everything for today. Has no one expressed their compliments?"

"To be fair, Lucy had a lot to do with the arrangements," Adriana countered.

"But from what I've seen, Roderick has her well in hand today."

"Yes, if he had his wish, she would be back at Aldred, not prancing around a dancefloor."

"Is she at risk?" Ellis asked immediately. "Has the doctor been to see her?"

"The doctor, several scholars, a midwife, an earl, a viscountess, and all the sisters-in-law," Adriana replied with a wide smile. "She is in her element and Roderick is trying desperately to maintain his balance, poor man. He'd like to wrap her in down pillows and keep all risk at further than arm's length, but he also doesn't want to take away her enjoyment of all the things." She laughed and shook her head before sighing and saying again, "Poor man."

"Don't pity him too much, he knew what he was doing when he wed her. She is a force to be reckoned with. But the doctor wasn't concerned?"

"Not overly, I don't think. Of course, as a maiden, most think I oughtn't be told anything of the matter, but he didn't appear grave at all when he took his leave. In fact, Roderick appeared to be reassured so I am convinced all is well. Also, Lucy promised Roderick she will cease her matchmaking for the time being and will accompany him back to the institute as soon as she has seen me off to my new position. A little something I haven't yet had a chance to thank you for, by the way."

To her delight the man actually blushed and yet one more thrill shivered through her.

"Oh, no, no thanks are needed at all. I assure you. I'm sure my cousins will be delighted with you."

Adriana managed not to laugh right in his face as he stammered out a reply, but it was a close-run thing for her. She had never seen him embarrassed and couldn't fathom why he would be so. Surely, he could take credit for settling her in a new position. One that appeared as though it would be quite delightful and not at all boring.

Not to say her other positions had been boring, not in the least. Her life with Mary had been lovely. There had been quiet moments, of course, which she didn't expect to exist in the household with seven girls, but Adriana hadn't known what boredom was until she had started to travel with Esther Bastion. But travel had been fascinating in its own way once you reached your destination. And her few days with Lady Evangeline had been harried and fascinating but not a second of restful. Adriana suspected she would quite enjoy her move to Beaverbrook, at least provided the girls didn't take her in dislike.

She had yet to meet them. She had only communicated through notes and letters with the oldest girl, who had seemed most personable in her writing, but what did that really say about anything? Lord Beaverbrook hadn't been terribly welcoming or even pleasant, but that could have been because of his very mixed feelings for his nephew who had made the introduction on the one brief afternoon that Eve had been able to spare her for the purpose.

It had been kind of the woman. Eve had sighed when Dria had broached the subject.

"I wish I could keep you," Evangeline had said with a wistful expression that bordered on regretful. "I want to keep you, of course, but I fear that it would be unfair to you to tell you I need you when you have this opportunity that could very well prove much better for you when I don't know if it will work out to keep you." Then she'd laughed. "That was not the least bit sensical was it?"

Despite the watery feeling in her throat, Adriana had laughed. "I understood completely what you were trying to convey and I deeply appreciate the sentiment. Thank you for not keeping me on a string when I can accept this new position. From what I understand, it took some doing to convince the earl that his daughters require my services so while I do think it will be a good position, I'm not completely certain of its stability."

"Promise me you'll come to me if it doesn't work out. Better yet, promise me you'll remain in touch with me even when you move to Beaverbrook. I might have hired you, but I still consider you to be my friend."

On an uncharacteristic impulse, Adriana had thrown her arms around the noblewoman and hugged her briefly. "I swear it," she had vowed with far more vehemence than was her usual behaviour.

"When do you join my cousins?" Ellis' question brought her back to the present, and Dria almost shook her head. She was in the most delicious moment of her life and she had been woolgathering. Obviously, she was losing her mind.

"Next week. Your uncle has promised to send a carriage for me. I hope he doesn't forget."

His clasp on her tightened slightly as though he too wished to pull her tighter. She dismissed the unhelpful, fanciful thought. The viscount shook his head. "The earl might be many things, but he isn't one to forget his word, not even when he is in his cups, and I'm certain he wouldn't have been sheets to the wind when meeting with you."

Adriana chuckled as the waltz wound to a conclusion, grateful for his distracting words to prevent her disappointment in the end of the dance from ruining her evening. "I cannot imagine the so proper gentleman doing something so ill bred."

"No, he contains his ill-bred behaviour to actions involving me, it would seem," Ellis replied cheerfully. "In any case, that merely means that he shan't forget you if he promised to send a carriage for you."

Adriana nodded and was about to take her leave of him when he asked her in an altered tone, "Did he mention his countess?"

Dria blinked and asked before she could catch herself, "Which one?" She nearly clamped a hand over her mouth in her discomfort as her eyes widened, but he only laughed and shook his head.

"That's a good question, not one to embarrass you, my dear. But I was referring to the one he thinks to wed. It's entirely possible he might have already done so."

"Would he not have told you? Would he not have wanted you there to witness the happy event?"

"No, I don't think he would. He is determined to unseat me from his succession, but he actually feels badly about that so in his mind having me there would feel akin to gloating."

Adriana frowned. "You wouldn't see it that way, though, would you?"

She couldn't interpret the delightful smile he cast her but he shook his head. "Of course not, but I can appreciate his sentiments nonetheless. I suspect, though, that was why he was so amenable to the idea of bringing you into the household. It is likely the new bride might not be much older than my first cousin. It will be more comfortable for everyone for you to take the girls in hand, which is exactly what I told my uncle."

"And once again, I must thank you for that."

"No thanks necessary, I will say again. And you really ought to reserve your judgment for after you've spent some time at Beaverbrook. What if you find it isn't to your taste?"

Adriana merely shook her head and smiled before taking her leave of the viscount quickly. How could she explain to him that she didn't have the luxury of liking or disliking her position? Because there were to be so many girls in her care, the earl had been generous in his offer to her. It was more than enough to keep her family satisfied and even set a little aside for herself for her own future. Not much, but it was better than she currently had, except for the few weeks where she had two employers.

She hurried away to check on the punch. Dithering wasn't likely to endear her to anyone.

Chapter Eighteen

Ellis watched the lovely woman walk briskly away.

Dancing with her had likely been a mistake. What was it about the woman that drew him so strongly? It was like the magnets one of the scholars had been working on. The ones that had been too strong to contain. That was how he felt when he was near Miss Adriana Adams. And according to his uncle, that was far from appropriate.

"Is that going to be a problem?"

Ellis could remember his uncle's scowl when he had been telling Beaverbrook about Miss Adams.

"Is what going to be a problem?"

"The girl's appeal?"

"How could you possibly know if she's appealing? You haven't even met her yet."

"I can hear it in your voice."

"You are mistaken, my lord. I am merely enthusiastic with my cousins, your daughters, in mind."

"Hmph," Beaverbrook had mumbled, unconvinced. "You are Viscount Severn. No nameless nobody will do for you, my boy."

Ellis had laughed and shaken his head. "You cannot have it both ways, Uncle. According to your wishes, I am a mere Mister Ellis Dorval, myself, in which case it won't matter who I wed with."

"You are still my dearest nephew, and if you are merely a mister you ought to find yourself a good heiress to marry, don't you think? If I manage to displace you, I might not be able to send you a quarterly anymore once the boy is older."

Ellis had merely laughed again and assured his uncle he needn't have any concerns about Miss Adams before he'd taken his leave of the earl. But watching her walk away with her determined but jaunty stride, Ellis wasn't so sure he had told his uncle the truth.

Not that it was any of his uncle's business who he involved himself with.

Beaverbrook couldn't disinherit him. That was proven. Unless the man fathered a son. Which he was trying quite studiously to do. Ellis shook his head and turned away. He ought to find Sean and congratulate the man.

He had to laugh when he found the mathematician in a huddle with some of the other scholars. They were talking about the treasure hunt. At the ball to celebrate Sean and Eve's wedding.

"If Lucy finds out, she'll have your hides," Ellis pointed out calmly, causing the others to start guiltily.

"But one of the fellows found another clue, and he's more convinced than ever that it's the lost library of Alexandria we're searching for," one scholar said, sounding defensive before adding, "But I wished for gems."

"You needn't explain yourself to me," Ellis said with a slight laugh over the scientist's disappointment. "I couldn't give a fig. But I suspect Sean ought to see to his new wife."

Sean laughed, seemingly not offended in the least. "Be sure to tell Adriana what was found," he said to the group before taking his leave. "Eve thinks she's more interested than she's let on, and she has a really detailed but succinct way of compiling notes. If we had the time, we'd make a scholar out of her," he added in a backward comment as he hurried off to lead his wife onto the dance floor.

Ellis watched with surprise flooding him. Adriana knew about the treasure hunt? Why had she never asked him about it? How had she found out?

He was being churlish to mind her involvement. And he didn't mind, he told himself. He just wished she had told him about it. Somehow it felt as though she were keeping secrets from him. Likely there was much he didn't know about the woman, he reminded himself. Perhaps he was just feeling possessive of the hunt, as though trying to keep it as a scholarly pursuit, not something to involve outsiders. Not to imply she was an outsider. Clearly he was muddled on the matter.

But he wished she had discussed it with him.

Ellis shook his head. When would she have been able to do that? During their dance? There hadn't been time, and it had been far too dreamy an experience to bring the ridiculous treasure hunt into it.

But perhaps not ridiculous. The other scholars seemed captivated by the subject and apparently had involved the companion. Of course, he had been out of Town for weeks, much had gone on without him, and he couldn't begrudge it to them.

He was going to profit wildly from his extraction technique, Ellis reminded himself. He didn't need the treasure in any way, whichever of their guesses proved to be correct. But he hated the feeling of being on the outside of a matter. He ought to have asked them a few questions to at least show his support. And he wouldn't mind to know what they had going on with their science either or even other aspects of life.

Not that anyone had asked him about where he had been the last weeks nor what he had been doing. Should he be offended? He wasn't. Did that make him strange? He was proud of himself and thrilled with the fact that he would be able to care for his own needs whether or not he remained Viscount Severn. He would happily tell anyone who asked him about it. And he had enjoyed discussing it in great detail with Roderick. But the only one he had voluntarily told anything about it was Adriana.

That was a rather alarming fact.

One he would have to think about later since he now needed to do as he had admonished the other scholars and return to the ball. Since there were so many of the studious sort at this particular social engagement, it would be terribly obvious and cause consternation to their hostess if they were to keep their heads tied up in scientific matters all evening.

Despite his lack of enthusiasm for the prospect, he ought to dance. And it would please his uncle were he to hear that Severn had partnered with some young ladies the earl would consider suitable. Not that it would mean anything. Ellis wasn't about to wed at his uncle's behest.

Especially not when that one was about to disinherit him. Ellis was only grateful throwing a ball after one wed was a rarity. Otherwise, he would have to do this all over again in the coming weeks, for Beaverbrook and his bride. Instead, now that Eve and Sean were safely wed, they could all return to the Institute and get back to normal. He was certainly looking forward to that. There was much he needed to do to further his business enterprises.

Chapter Nineteen

Before she could catch her breath from the wedding, Adriana found herself bowling along a reasonably well-maintained road in a quite comfortable carriage, trying to examine her feelings. Relief was one of them, she supposed. Relief that the earl had remembered his promise to send for her whether he was in residence or not. There hadn't been any notes or messages for her, but the crest on the carriage had been the right one and the Northcott servants had assured her she could safely accept the transport on offer. She was also deeply, intensely tired. It had been a rather ridiculous month full of errands and learning new things and trying to juggle obligations to two different employers. It had been exhilarating, besides, but it wasn't an experience Adriana would wish to repeat despite the fact that she could now look back on it with a degree of satisfaction. The coins jingling in her reticule was part of the satisfaction.

Evangeline had created an account for her at her bank and put all Dria's wages there rather than sending any to the Adams family. And she had spoken sternly to Adriana about ensuring she kept some of the wages she would be receiving from Lord Beaverbrook in the future.

"Your family needn't know all the details of your employment, Dria. You are an adult now. It is really a private matter. If you choose to send them some of your wages, that is your personal affair. But all your matters from here on out are your own affairs. You don't owe explanations to anyone. Not your family, and not me, either," she added with a light laugh as she was taking her leave. "But swear to me that you will remain in contact, as well as promise you'll come to me if you run into any difficulties in the future."

As she arrived at the rather austere property she suspected must be the home of the Earl of Beaverbrook, Adriana swallowed the lump that threatened to cut off her breath. Thinking about friends she was going to miss wasn't going to help her settle into her new circumstances. She pushed the thoughts aside and followed the footman into the house.

Moments later, Adriana tried to keep up as the young woman escorted her up the flights of stairs. She was surprised the young ladies of the home were being kept so far from the usual space for the family. But maybe it was just the nursery. Dria didn't ask questions, merely trying not to get left behind as the young woman who introduced herself as Cordelia strode swiftly up the stairs.

"The others are very excited to meet you. They've never met a companion before. Nor a woman of Society who hasn't been married to our father. I trust you shan't be overwhelmed by their eager welcome."

Dria frowned. *They'd never met other ladies? How perfectly odd. Were they much younger than she had been led to believe? Why had their mothers not introduced them to other children of the gentry in the neighborhood?* It took a surprising amount of effort to keep all her questions within the confines of her own mind. It wouldn't do to pelt the young woman with questions, even if Dria thought she would be able to do so and keep her breath as they continued to climb.

So far, from what Adriana could see, the house was well-run. A groom had been waiting for her when the carriage had arrived and he had quickly collected her baggage and had her on the way into the house without delay. The housekeeper and butler had greeted her, seemingly with enthusiastic delight while a footman had dashed away to "collect Lady Cordelia," as Mrs. Sparks, the housekeeper had said.

As they climbed the stairs, Adriana noted the cleanliness of what she could see. There were servants bustling about with cleaning materials. She watched in a state of fascination that caused her footsteps to falter as a pair of footmen set up a ladder to clean the chandelier in the soaring entryway.

"Why do they not just lower it?" Dria asked the girl she was hurrying behind once they were out of earshot.

"They want to inspect the pulley system. It seems to have developed a squeak."

It took effort for Adriana not to turn back to watch some more. Clearly her time with the Scholarly Society had affected her desire to know how things worked. But for now, she had people to consider. How was she going to manage seven of them? She had thought two were a challenge.

But the younger ones would have their governess, likely even more than one, she assured herself as they finally gained the top of the last flight of stairs. Adriana was rewarded with a small smile of approval from the young lady. Perhaps the mad dash up the stairs had been a test. Adriana wasn't offended, but she was amused. Oddly enough it helped quell her nerves.

"Are you ready?" Cordelia asked with a slight frown. Adriana wasn't left to wonder what the woman was thinking. "The timing of your arrival couldn't have been better," she said. "While you aren't responsible for the little girls just yet, I hope you won't mind their wish to spend some time with you. There are very mixed feelings about our father's marriage."

It seemed like two disparaging thoughts, but Adriana realized Cordelia was trying to tell her that the youngest children were likely hurt or saddened by the earl replacing their mother so quickly. Ellis had told her that the earl was barely waiting out the year before taking a new wife. It was unlikely the youngest of his daughters would even remember their mother, she thought with a slight stutter in the region of her heart. Poor little muffins.

Neither Viscount Severn nor the girls' father had told Adriana the exact ages of her new companions. She wondered if either of them even knew. But if she had to guess, she would put Cordelia's age around seventeen or eighteen, possibly even nineteen. The girl would be eligible for her first Season one of these days soon. Dria supposed the other six girls would be staggered in age behind Cordelia. She wondered how close and where the gaps were. She knew there had been two mothers, the earl's first and second wives. And now he was about to take on a third. All in the hopes that he could have a son.

Adriana pasted a smile onto her face that she hoped was sincere and interested, not sympathetic and melancholy, as she entered the room on Cordelia's heels, feeling prepared to meet the girls and get on with things. Even without having met them yet, she was already well on her way to giving the sisters her heart.

The room was eerily quiet as eight pairs of eyes stared at her without comment. Adriana tried to follow along as Cordelia introduced her sisters.

"That's Seraphina, Lavinia, and Amelia," she said pointing, and then adding, "Here's Penelope, Prudence, and our baby Primrose."

"Not a baby," the little girl said with a pout. She wasn't an infant but she couldn't be much more than two, really barely even able to voice her objections to the word. Adriana watched with interest as the girl's thumb slipped into her mouth before the attentive nursemaid pulled the child's hand away.

"I'm very pleased to make your acquaintance," Adriana said with a small curtsy to the room at large. She might be their paid companion and several years older than them, but they were the daughters of an earl, whether he wanted them or not.

Suddenly, the quiet was broken as the younger girls all began to pelt her with questions. She wasn't able to answer a single one as they were all speaking over each other.

"Girls, girls," the tall thin woman Adriana assumed was their governess called out in a calm, steady voice that seemed to break through the tumult. "Did I not teach you better than this?"

"Sorry, Miss Plum," Penelope said, hanging her head down in a semblance of shame, but Dria could see the mischievous smile peeping between the plaits of the girl's hair. Dria bit the inside of her cheek slightly to keep a smile off her own face. It wouldn't be good to support insubordination of the youngsters toward their governess. But Adriana realized she was going to find much to amuse her in her new life.

"Is anyone comfortable telling me their ages?" Adriana asked, breaking the strained silence that had followed the governess' correction.

"I'm three," the youngest said, holding up a pudgy hand with three fingers extended. Cordelia had identified her as Primrose if Adriana remembered correctly.

The rest of the younger girls followed suit. "Six," "Eight," "I'm almost ten." Adriana had nearly laughed over that one. "Twelve," said a shy voice from a small girl. Adriana would have thought she was about the same age as the jester Penelope. Of course, she wouldn't remark upon it out loud. Her gaze shifted to the two oldest girls – Cordelia and her sister Seraphina. Neither seemed nearly as anxious as the younger girls to say much, especially not announcing their years.

"Sera just turned sixteen and Cordelia is going to be nineteen next week," Amelia added in her small, shy voice.

"Thank you, Amelia," Adriana replied politely, watching the silent communication among the sisters. She suspected Seraphina would be her biggest challenge. She seemed to be the one most mired in resentment. Why, Dria couldn't be sure. But she didn't think it was specifically personal toward her. She suspected the girl was resentful of everyone. Dria couldn't really blame her; she was actually surprised more of the girls didn't act similarly considering what she knew of their father's treatment of them.

After that, they settled in quite nicely. Adriana quickly felt at home with the girls and easily found her way around the very large house. It wasn't hard to grow to love all seven of the girls, even the prickly Seraphina. She tried not to encourage them to do so, but Adriana couldn't help the leap her heart took every time the girls spoke of their cousin, Severn.

One thing that surprised her, though, was that they made very little mention of their father's upcoming marriage nor their feelings about his new wife. Dria wondered how the young countess' presence in the house would affect her own status.

It delighted her that she had so few spare moments to worry, a skill she was most adept at when she had too much time on her hands. When she did find herself with a bit of time, rather than obsessing over what she had no control over, she easily filled it with staying in touch with the scholars and writing to anyone they thought might have leads on the treasure. The scholars had connected her with some contacts at Oxford and she had already established a correspondence. That meant more individuals with whom they would have to split the treasure once they finally found it, but there was nothing to be done about that.

Even though she didn't feel as anxious about her future, now that she was settled in at Beaverbrook, no position could truly be considered secure, so she continued sharing in the pursuit of the unknown, hopefully lucrative, treasure and the clues the scholars came up with from time to time.

It brought slivers of delight into her rather narrow life whenever she heard from the scholars. She was grateful they remembered about her in what felt almost like a self-imposed exile after her more active or exciting life with Miss Bastion and then briefly Lady Evangeline and the Northcotts.

We got news from a woman at Oxford, the daughter of one of our professors. She's found one of the surviving books from the Popery Purge. We think it might be where Lady E's husband's first clue came from, a missing page from the book. But Pierce thought Faith, the professor's daughter, would be more comfortable corresponding with you. So you'll be our go-between, if that's fine with you.

Adriana had almost laughed out loud when she'd read that note from Jasper, one of the other scholars. As if she wouldn't be fine with it. For one thing, making the acquaintance of another interesting young woman would be a delight, for another, staying involved in the search, even from a distance, made her feel a part of things.

Of course, she was a part of things here at Beaverbrook. Trying to have a care to the seven sisters' fragile feelings made her feel more valuable than she ever had in her life.

But despite that it was a rather ordinary existence.

Even when the new Countess Beaverbrook moved in, nothing really changed in the companion's life. The young Lady Beaverbrook took her lead from her husband and barely acknowledged the nursery or the occupants of it. Adriana considered it very odd that she and the older girls weren't invited to take tea with the countess or in any way acknowledged by her unless they were to encounter her in the hallways of the large house, which didn't happen very often.

Without ever being explicitly told, somehow Adriana was brought to understand that she and her charges were not invited into the more public parts of the house. If they were ever thought of, the lord and lady came to the nursery, not the other way around. It didn't seem to bother the sisters aside from their discomfort when it seemed they were being inspected by their new stepmother, which only happened very rarely. Adriana kept her own thoughts on the matter to herself.

They took to spending much time out of doors, wandering the fields and dales of the large estate. Adriana broached the subject of pin money with the earl when she had finally been able to arrange an audience with him.

"Why would the girls need any ready blunt? Just have their bills sent to me."

"But what about picking out ribbons in the shops or taking tea or some such? Should they not be entrusted with a small amount of spending money so they can learn how to conduct themselves? At least the older girls ought to do so. Otherwise, how will they manage when they make their debut?"

It was evident this thought had never occurred to the earl but after some unintelligible grumbling, he agreed. "But you distribute it to them, Miss Adams, I don't want them presenting themselves to me with their hands out forever after this."

“Very well. Shall we say on the first of each month I shall make an accounting with you or would you prefer I see the steward about the matter?”

“Oh, yes, you’re a wise girl, that is a sound suggestion. The steward will handle it. I will mention it to him when next we meet. Thank you, Miss Adams.”

He had handed her a small sack she was nearly certain contained some funds but she didn’t want to open it in his presence. She had merely bobbed a respectful curtsy and made her escape. As soon as she had been able, she had called Seraphina and Cordelia to her room and they had opened it together.

“I spoke to your father about us making some excursions into the village. It was clear it had never occurred to him that you ought to do so. But how else are you to learn to converse with strangers or negotiate purchases? The three of us will begin right away, but I think we ought to include some of the other girls once we’ve gone a couple of times ourselves.”

“Oh, Miss Adriana,” Cordelia had breathed in awe, reverting to a more polite address as a way to express her shock and amazement. “I do swear you must have mystical powers. I would never have thought to ask my father for pin money, let alone have any expectation that he would say yes.”

“I think the lot of you girls ought to make a greater effort to include your father in your lives. It seems to me he isn’t such a terrible fellow.”

Seraphina had merely snorted over Dria’s words while she continued to count the money the earl had provided. Suddenly and uncharacteristically, she laughed.

“I don’t know why we are oohing and aahing over these coins, Cordelia. It isn’t as though we even have a concept of what they can do for us.”

“It is what they symbolize. We will learn. And we have Adriana to thank for it,” she said firmly before turning to that good woman with a giggle. “Can we go straight away?”

“I think we ought to wait until morning. Since neither of you have ever gone, we cannot even say for certain how long it will take us. Should we ask at the stables for a gig or horses or try to walk ourselves? I passed through the village on the way here, but I didn’t think to remark how far it might have been.” She paused for a moment. “I will confer with Mrs. Parks this evening. She or the butler will know what we ought to do.”

“They shan’t believe you managed it,” Cordelia crowed while Adriana only shook her head even as her own excitement grew to match the others’.

Chapter Twenty

Ellis spent the next few months pursuing his business. His uncle wrote to him repeatedly about his lowly activities. The latest had just arrived.

Severn,

You must cease this humiliating pursuit of business at once. It is because of your association with that woman who wed your friend, isn't it? You are all trying to make your families a laughing stock. How can we hold our heads up in public if our relations are turning into cits? I know you are likely proud of yourself for inventing something but selling it for profit is humiliating.

You must come for your quarterly visit as soon as possible and we can discuss it in person. I might be a father again soon. The suspense is making me near to perishing. Might be the boy I've always wanted.

I will disinherit you if you don't uphold the family name better than this, Severn.

Yours,
Beaverbrook

Ellis shook his head. If his uncle could disinherit him, he would have done it long before now, so he was well aware that threat was empty. Of course, the man could cut off his allowance, but that no longer mattered. His income from the extraction processing device was now far larger than what his stingy uncle had ever allotted to him.

He was worried about his cousins and even his new aunt, and he ought to visit to see how they all went on, but he worried about his feelings for the companion. It had seemed like a good idea when he had suggested it, but now Adriana's presence at Beaverbrook made him want to stay away for fear of giving his heart even more. The earl wasn't the only one who wrote to him.

> *Dear Cousin Ellis,*
>
> *Thank you for sending us our dear Adriana. She has helped all the girls to brighten up about Father's new wife. Even Seraphina likes her, I think. It's hard to tell with her, you know. But Adriana talks of taking me for my debut. I didn't think I would ever want to leave the other girls but if she stays, I feel as though I can. It would be lovely to have a home of my own, but I fear leaving the little ones.*
>
> *Do you think any gentleman would want to wed with a lady who came with the possibility of needing to take in six or more sisters? It surely would be daunting to any man. But Adriana assures me there will be gentlemen who would consider it an honour. Isn't that the kindest thing you've ever heard of?*
>
> *Amelia has started wearing her hair the same way as Adriana and the little girls are trying to speak just like her. I think Miss Plum might be jealous but she's trying to take it well. There is*

certainly more harmony in the nursery since Adriana arrived.

Did Father tell you the countess was increasing right away? I hesitate to mention such a topic, of course. But the sad thing is she lost it pretty quickly. It made me wonder if she hadn't really been increasing at all and only told him that for reasons of her own. I don't know her very well, of course, so I shouldn't speculate. Adriana says it must be a challenge to come into a household such as ours as the new wife and I ought to try to sympathize with her ladyship's plight. I know she's right but it's a challenge for me to look at it that way. Adriana says challenges make us grow.

Prim wants to start schooling already. Isn't that darling? She says it's so that she can write to you herself. But in the meantime, she will send her greetings through me. But stay ever hopeful of receiving a missive from the youngest of your cousins shortly. While you wait, I'm sure the other girls will be sending you their news. Except for Sera. She's still caught up in her personal despair.

I do not have any true news to share with you aside from the fact that Adriana insisted I start learning everything that will be required of a debutante. We have all started to learn the steps of the dances. Adriana says it's a shame I haven't been taught before but that all the girls ought to learn. So she and Miss Plum demonstrate and we all get ourselves into stitches of laughter. Mayhap you could come and partner with them to really show us how it is done. Surely, you're due for a visit soon.

We await your arrival with bated breath,

Your servant and loving cousin,
Cordelia

With a sigh, Ellis put the letter down on his desk and wondered if he ought to discuss the matter with Lucy and Roderick. But knowing Lucy's determination to matchmake he didn't think it would be a good idea. Besides, he was a scientist, a scholar, surely he could keep his feelings out of the situation and rationally visit with his family without fear for the safety of his heart.

He had several reasons for which he ought to visit Beaverbrook. For one thing, he hadn't yet met the new countess and it had already been several months. He also hadn't visited his uncle's properties or seen his cousins. Neither were truly his responsibility, his uncle was still very much alive, but he had promised his cousins he would do a better job of staying active in their lives than he had been doing. He was determined to keep that promise. And from Cordelia's letter, it didn't sound as though this countess was any different from the last one in her involvement with Beaverbrook's daughters.

This left him to wonder if it was the earl's choice that his wife ignore the girls or if it was normal female behavior. Also evident from Cordelia's letter, Miss Adams wasn't ignoring any of the girls despite the fact that she had only been hired to be companion to the oldest two. But she wasn't their stepmother, not that Ellis thought it was an acceptable excuse, but he was sure it did make a difference in the household dynamics.

From veiled hints in earlier messages from Beaverbrook, Ellis suspected the new countess might have already lost one pregnancy. Perhaps it had only been wishful thinking on the earl's part that she was even increasing in the first place. They hadn't been wed for long. But he now thought she might be again.

What happened to their agreement that she only be expected to become pregnant once a year? Ellis had wondered how such a promise could be enforced when Beaverbrook had told him of it. If his suspicions were correct, it would seem he had been right. Of course, it might just be the wily earl's machinations to try to control his current heir's actions by telling him there was a new heir on the way. Or perhaps the man had negotiated the agreement to be different in the first year or two. Since they hadn't yet been wed for long, as Cordelia said, the first suspected pregnancy might have been wishful thinking.

Whatever the case, Ellis needed to make a trip to the earl's main seat to see for himself what the situation is with his family members. A man of science should not allow his actions to be controlled by something so nebulous as feelings. He couldn't stay away because of how attractive he found his cousins' companion. How foolish would that be? And he would never admit to being a fool.

With a sigh and a nod, he wrote a note and called a footman to have it delivered to his uncle before calling his valet to pack for him. He needed to take care of his responsibilities before he returned to the scholarly estate. He didn't need to discuss these things with the Northcotts. Surely as a businessman and a man of science he could manage to make a rational decision on such a matter.

Chapter Twenty-One

Adriana had settled quite nicely into her new life as the paid companion to the seven young women, or rather paid companion to two and loving associate of five more. It was a far cry from her life with either Mary or Esther but she found she quite loved it. Similar to the life she and Mary lived, Dria supposed, but far busier with the seven girls to keep life interesting. And she was enjoying the respite from the High Society that Miss Bastion, or rather Lady Droitmuir, had loved.

Dria was pleased to hear regularly from a few of the women in her past, though. It would make launching her girls easier when the time came. Staying at least a little in touch with her acquaintances would mean she was somewhat up to date on the goings on as well as having connections for making calls and arranging invitations. She was trying to prepare both Lady Cordelia and Seraphina for their debuts. They were still trying to decide if Cordelia ought to debut on her own or wait until Sera was ready to join her and they could go together.

"I'm of two minds, really, Dria," Cordelia said on a dramatic sigh. "I'm afraid Sera will end up refusing to go to Town altogether and then I will have waited for nothing. But having grown quite accustomed to all my sisters, won't it be quite strange to enter Society without at least one of them by my side?"

"Only you can decide that, I'm afraid," Adriana said. "I can understand why you would like the company of your sisters, but of course, I will be by your side so you shan't be completely alone. Not the same as a sister, I know," she added with a self-deprecating smile.

"Oh, no, I'm a beast," Cordelia exclaimed running to launch herself at the companion. "I meant you no insult at all, dearest Dria. You shall be perfect, to be sure."

Adriana laughed. "I wasn't insulted, dearest. But how do you truly feel about making your debut? Do you wish to remain here a few years longer? There isn't a rush, you aren't so terribly long in the tooth."

Cordelia sighed again, this one sounding genuine and slightly disconsolate. "I was being truthful when I said I am of two minds. A part of me fears I shan't take so I might need a couple chances to find my match. And do I really want to leave these six and go out into the unknown? On the other hand, I have these six to think about. What if our father changes his mind on sponsoring the lot of us? What if his new wife convinces him we're too much trouble? If I am wed, I can take everyone after me into my home or at least to Town for matches of their own. I hate the thought of leaving my sisters even for the weeks of the Season, but especially on a more permanent basis, but what if it's the only way to ensure they have a safe and secure future?"

Adriana wished she could assure the girl that she needn't take on the responsibility for her sisters' futures but from what she had seen thus far in her weeks at Beaverbrook, she was right in thinking there were no guarantee of what the earl and his countess might do.

The new countess was polite enough but terribly young and seemed to feel her position was threatened by everyone and everything. It occurred to Adriana the girl might feel more confident if she were to finally bear the earl his son, but then where would that leave the current Viscount Severn?

She tried not to think about Ellis. While he was her charges' cousin, he wasn't anything to her and she really shouldn't allow him to occupy any part of her mind or heart or thoughts or time. But she couldn't seem to help herself. She thought of the handsome chemist often and wondered how he was doing with the invention he had told her about.

With a shake of her head, Adriana tried to dismiss thoughts of the man from her conscious thought. She needed to focus on the girls and their need for attention and direction.

Seraphina came into the room. "We were just thinking about you," Adriana told the girl with a gentle smile as she settled into her favorite seat in the room they had turned into their sitting room. Adriana had been rather shocked to realize the girls were still confined to the nursery when she had arrived and had seen to the arrangements soon after.

Sera made a sound that was almost a grunt, not bothering to reply to Adriana's statement. This prompted a frown from her sister and a puff of laughter from her companion.

"Perhaps that answers our question without even needing to ask it. Whether you want to or not is a moot point if you're going to sound like an animal."

"What are you talking about?" Seraphina demanded with a grimace.

"We were just discussing whether or not Cordelia ought to delay her debut so that she can do it with you, but we weren't sure if you will be ready by next year."

Sera's face flooded with a mixture of dismay and embarrassment, surprising Adriana. Had they hurt the girl's feelings?

"We didn't mean it as a disparagement, but you don't seem the least bit eager to go to Town. Cordelia, though, isn't fully comfortable with the thought of going with just me as company when she's so used to having many sisters around."

"Delia," Sera said with exasperation. "You know it isn't natural to have so many girls around. You should be thrilled to have some quiet time alone. I know I would be."

"We all know you and I are very different although I love you dearly," Cordelia countered with a dry tone.

"Would you consider coming to Town with us, even if you didn't officially make your debut?" Adriana asked Seraphina.

"How do you mean?" The younger girl appeared intrigued with the idea.

"The three of us could take up residence in London, maybe at your father's townhouse or, if he would prefer, we could rent rooms. Then you could accompany us as we explore the city but if you didn't feel ready to make your debut, you needn't attend the social events, especially not the evening ones like balls and routs and such."

Cordelia clapped her hands with delight while even Seraphina seemed pleased with the idea.

"Is that even possible?" Sera asked with widened eyes and the most interest she had shown in anything since Adriana had arrived on the estate.

"Of course. I would say anything is possible. But certainly this. That is if your father approves. But it would give you a little bit of polish before you made your own debut. And would make the prospect of debuting on your own a little less daunting for each of you."

"Why would I debut on my own?" Seraphina asked with a frown.

"Well, I would be with you, of course, but if Cordelia finds a match in her first Season, that would leave you to either debut alone or wait several years until Lavinia is ready."

"Ah, I see," the girl said with a frown that Adriana interpreted to mean she hadn't thought of that development. There was a pause of silence before she turned her intelligent gaze upon her companion. "What do you think I should do?"

"I think you should plan to come with us to Town. It'll help Cordelia be more comfortable and even help the younger girls grow accustomed to what the future may hold. If you hate it, you can come home. If you love it, you'll stay with us. You could even make a partial debut if you like it well enough. But in either case, it will make you more used to it. If you then decide to wait for Lavinia, you'll at least feel a little more comfortable when you eventually do go back."

The girl nodded as though in deep contemplation. "I really never thought there was a middle possibility like that. And you're right, it would be better for me to see for myself what all the fuss is about. I would dearly love to see the various collections I've heard about, like Elgin's marbles."

Cordelia reached over and grasped Adriana's hand as though to thank her. Dria's heart clenched. She was trying her best for the girls and was thrilled they were appreciative. All she wanted to do was be of assistance to them.

"We can ask Severn about it when he comes, too," Cordelia said, making Adriana's heart clench in a different way. She had to cough to cover the sensation that her heart had skipped a beat.

"Oh, is he coming?" she asked weakly.

"Well, he has to, eventually. He is still Viscount Severn, at least for now." This was from Sera, and Adriana tried not to flinch or react in any visible way. She had begun to allow herself to exhibit more of her own feelings and reactions while in company with the earl's daughters but that only served to make it harder for her to hide her feelings when she really needed to. Like now.

"I think he'll be here soon. He missed his last quarterly visit, which was particularly odd considering he had just promised us he would do better," Cordelia mused. "I was expecting him to visit more, not less. But he does write." The last bit sounded grudging to Adriana's ears.

Adriana didn't want to add to the conversation but couldn't seem to help herself. The urge to defend the charismatic chemist was hard to ignore.

"Is it possible that he felt he had sent me in his stead?"

Cordelia laughed. "Oh, certainly possible, especially as it pertains to us girls, but he has almost never, in all the years I've known him, missed his quarterly visit with Father and the stewards."

Adriana made a noncommittal noise and turned the subject, determined to ignore the flutter of anticipation in her midsection. If he did come, she would manage. She always managed.

Cordelia's prediction turned out to be accurate. They heard from the housekeeper the next day that Severn had written to inform Beaverbrook he would be visiting that week. Adriana wondered for a wild moment if she ought to take some time off.

It had been her original intention, when she had realized she had some extra funds from her time working for two very different women as their companions. She had meant to go on her own to the seaside or some other perfectly acceptable trip for a young woman on her own. But the opportunity to be companion for the Beaverbrook daughters had been too much of a draw for her to ignore, so she had come straight away rather than after a holiday. But now might be a good time to rectify that omission.

Except that she couldn't leave her girls.

They had made their way into her heart and taken up residence. She couldn't leave them when they would need her most. With their new stepmother in residence and yet keeping to herself, life felt uneasy for the sisters, Adriana knew. She wasn't going to add to that discomfort.

So, she would just ignore any discomfort the viscount's presence might cause her. She was quite used to ignoring her own discomfort. As a paid companion, she had been doing that for years. It was a well-worn habit, just shoving the thoughts and feelings away. They didn't matter and wouldn't benefit her in any way. Certainly, feeling attracted to a titled gentleman was less than helpful to her circumstances.

Adriana was grateful she had been given warning, at least to a certain degree, so that she didn't have a fit of the vapours, despite the impulse to give into such a riotous reaction that was completely unusual for her, when she ran across Viscount Severn suddenly in the hallway two days later.

"How do you do?" she managed to ask politely, with barely a flicker of an eyelash.

"Very well, thank you for asking," he replied politely before stepping much too close and taking her hand, bowing over it gallantly before turning her hand over and placing a kiss gently on the inside of her wrist.

It felt as though her entire body went up in flames, which was far more dramatic a reaction than she had ever experienced. With a stifled sigh she ignored the intense sensation and dipped a slight curtsy to the gentleman. But then she turned on her heel and literally ran away.

She never would have thought herself capable of being so craven. But despite all her attestations to the contrary, she had not prepared herself well for encountering the very handsome and oh so appealing Ellis Dorval, Viscount Severn, in his uncle's hallway.

"Whatever has happened?" Lady Cordelia exclaimed when Dria burst into the schoolroom where, as usual, the girls were gathered.

"Oh, lawks, naught," Adriana said airily as she picked up little Lady Primrose and twirled her about the room thus stirring up hilarity amongst the youngsters and pushing all other thoughts from her head.

Chapter Twenty-Two

After spending an entire day sequestered with the steward, reviewing the ledgers, and riding over the land, Ellis spent a delightful evening with his cousins. Well, it ought to have been delightful except that with the beautiful but silent presence of their companion, it was something akin to torture when all he really wanted to do was discuss everything with her.

She had excused herself early when the youngest took to their beds, leaving him with Seraphina and Cordelia. He was both disappointed and relieved.

"So tell me truthfully, ladies, how do you go on?"

"We haven't been trying to pull the wool over your eyes, Severn, we are very well. You did us the greatest service when you sent our dear Adriana to us. She has managed to make Father's remarriage and the presence of a new countess as nothing." Cordelia paused and exchanged a glance with her sister.

After a light laugh, she elaborated. "Dria wouldn't want us to say it was nothing. Rather it isn't something that injures us in any way." She paused again, and Ellis waited to see if she was finished.

With a puff of what might have been frustration, she explained further. "Our mothers are dead. I believe ours, mine and Sera's and Livie and Amelia, I mean, she truly cared for us, from what I can remember of her. The second countess was too tired, I think, to take any interest in us. Even our own countess mother, I think, by the end of her life, she barely visited the nursery or schoolroom. This one will be no different. But we have each other. If there are more girls, we will love them too, of course. They will be our sisters. If there is a brother born, finally, that might change everything. Or it might not. There's really no way to know how the earl or his wife will react to finally having a son. To be sure, the earl will rejoice. But whether or not it will have any effect on our lives, it's really unlikely at this point. In fact, it could be argued, the countess could become more certain of herself and her place in the household. It is very likely she would ensure that we vacate the premises. So I think Dria is right. I need to make my debut and ensure I'm in a position to care for my sisters in the future."

Ellis wanted to leave it at that, but he knew he owed them more. Despite his urge to leave the property as quickly as possible, in order to avoid his growing but terribly inconvenient feelings for the companion, he had to ensure his cousins were truly well.

"How do you feel about that? It's a large obligation for someone so young," he added, watching as the two girls exchanged silent communication once more.

To his amazement Cordelia shrugged. "It isn't such a large obligation, I don't think. Adriana is starting to train us in what we ought to know about managing a property and how to go to shops and such. From what I can tell, as long as I wed someone with sufficient status and wealth, there will be servants to help with anything and everything. I will just have to give some sort of nominal direction. Really, nothing need change in how my life carries on."

Ellis laughed. "A maiden companion might not be in the best position to teach you about your future married life."

Cordelia blushed and laughed along with him. "No, I suppose not, but even observing our father's wives has shown me I'm not that far off the mark. Of course, there would be children, hopefully. I would never allow them to be locked away in the attics like we have been. But I cannot see that being a wife is such an arduous task unless you cannot bear a son. Then you might die. But Dria has assured me that ladies all over the realm manage to bear sons without much trouble nearly every day of the week. Else the nation would expire."

Ellis laughed again and just shook his head. He wasn't about to add to his cousin's worries by trying to explain anything to the contrary to her.

"I'm glad you have taken to her," was all he bothered to say.

The next day he sought out the object of his obsession. The delectable but off-limits Miss Adams.

"I hear you are working wonders with my cousins."

"Oh, surely not wonders, my lord," she said with a negligent wave of her hand, looking about her as though for a means of escape.

"Do stay a moment, please, Adriana. Are we not friends? I would dearly like to discuss matters with you."

This drew her up short, and she returned to the stoically polite woman he had known in Town. Even though he had found that creature to be delightful, he found the more animated woman his cousins knew to be even more enticing. But he couldn't dwell upon that at the moment.

"Really, how are my cousins?"

"Truly, Ellis," she said, following his suit of informality. "They are well. Have you not asked them for yourself?"

"Well, of course I have, but I cannot quite be satisfied with the answers I have been given. Tell me what you have done. They seem quite content with your company."

She turned a little pink at his words. "Thank you for saying so. I am delighted with theirs, I must say." She laughed a little and shook her head. "I cannot say that I have done anything out of the ordinary except provide them with company as I have been hired to do. I don't know if you will credit this, though, but it seems they have not had any company aside from governesses through the years. The last countess never invited them to the withdrawing room when she was receiving, and they have never been taken into the village. It is a wonder they are not little savages, every last one of them. I suppose your uncle saw fit to employ proper governesses, so they have been taught how to go on, but you wouldn't believe the delight Cordelia and Seraphina take in the simplest thing like picking out ribbons in the village shop. We are to start taking the younger girls with us from time to time once the older ones grow more accustomed to speaking with strangers and bargaining. We are of a mind to make it a reward of sorts for good behaviour or learning something. We haven't reached a conclusion as of yet, but that is the thought."

Ellis shook his head even as he fought the urge to reach out and caress Adriana's cheek. It was a strange compulsion, not one he had ever experienced before. He managed to ignore it, barely.

"Thank you for doing that," he choked out, focusing on their conversation.

"Please, no thanks are necessary. I am merely amazed that it is such a novelty in this household. But they are all bright and quick girls, they will learn everything they ought to know very quickly. I am certain Cordelia will be ready for her debut when she decides to make it."

"And you are determined to remain with them?"

"But of course, where else would I be?"

"You had dreamed of taking a holiday," he pointed out.

She nodded but then quickly shook her head. "I had, you're right. I've almost forgotten. But this is better than a holiday, I think. What would I do all by myself? It would be most strange. And here, out in the country, it is nearly idyllic to my way of thinking. And there is never a dull moment with seven lovely girls to keep company with."

"What of wedding?"

"Who? Cordelia? That will happen, of course, and we will all miss her dreadfully, but then, if his lordship sees fit, my company will transfer to Lavinia in addition to Seraphina, and on and on. I will be well occupied for years to come. We will be desperately saddened to marry off each girl, one by one, of course, but that is the usual way of things in a regular family, is it not?"

"I spoke of your wedding," he said quietly, his low tone clearly flustering her as hectic colour splashed up onto her cheeks.

"That is not for me, my lord, and you oughtn't to tease me thusly. I have your dear cousins to see to now. My dearest wish is to be needed. And they do need me, I am certain of that."

"A husband would need you just as much or even more," he said, amazed at his persistence and calm.

"Where is this potential bridegroom, then?" she asked, becoming a little shrill. "And why would you speak like this to me when you arranged for me to be here?"

"You could wed with me, and we could take my cousins with us to Severn." He blurted the words as though they had ripped themselves from behind his teeth.

It was probably much too soon for her to accept such an offer, but he couldn't seem to help himself. She stared at him without blinking or saying a word, and it urged him to further declarations.

"I cannot think you are indifferent to me, Adriana. And I can assure you I have very warm feelings for you in return. Surely you realize this. Beaverbrook has told me his wife is increasing. He is quite convinced this time it is to be the son he has always longed for."

"Well then Severn won't be for you, will it? And this is all an empty conversation."

"But I did it! I finally finished my extraction contraption and have heaps of income. We can find a property for the lot of us, you, me and my cousins, and it will be even better than here." She continued to stare at him. It drove him to desperation. "Can you honestly say you haven't thought of it? Do you not have at least a little feeling for me, Adriana?"

To his shock, tears welled up in her eyes. "It matters not one jot that I have warm feelings for you, Mr. Dorval or Lord Severn, or whoever you might be. I am your cousins' companion. Their father is still very much alive and in charge of their lives. It is most inappropriate for us to have this conversation. And I will ask you not to press it upon me any longer."

Without another word she ran away from him once more. It didn't convince Ellis that she had no feelings for him, but it was true that it was highly irregular for him to press his advances upon his cousins' companion. Perhaps she will have warmed to the idea by his next quarterly visit. The thought didn't quite console him, but it would have to do. At least he knew she wasn't likely to find someone else to wed in the meantime.

But his heart was heavy as he left the estate. The next quarter was going to drag by, he was sure.

Chapter Twenty-Three

Adriana took a deep breath before she opened the door to the schoolroom. The noise coming from behind the closed door sounded so normal, exactly what she had heard every day for the months of her stay here at Beaverbrook. But how could they sound so normal?

The Earl and Countess of Beaverbrook were dead.

It was hard to believe. That poor young woman had been so excited about her pregnancy. Dria wasn't sure if it was her first or second, but at least the current one had seemed to be real. It had been evident the lady was increasing. But she had wanted to see her parents before her confinement. She had insisted the earl take her. The weather had been perfectly fine when they had set out, but from what Adriana had been able to piece together from the speculation of the servants, a storm had brewed as they had neared the North Downs. Dria hadn't thought they were high enough to generate any sort of varied weather. But then again, what did she really know of the matter?

Whatever the case, it would seem they must have thought they were so near their destination, they might as well press on. That had obviously been a mistake. The horses had lost their footing, possibly frightened by a gust of wind coming up the cliff, who could say at this point, but the broken carriage had been found at the bottom of a shallow cliff the next morning with the earl and his wife dead inside. One of the horses had surprisingly survived the fall despite the carriage's destruction.

Now the household was in mourning. Everything was in an uproar. Well, not everything. Perhaps that was only the chaos Adriana was trying to control from within her own mind. The girls took it in their stride as though it mattered little.

And Viscount Severn was now the Earl of Beaverbrook.

That was what had Dria in a tizzy. The new earl would be arriving any minute, she was sure.

If only she had managed to find the treasure they had been searching for. Then she could be gone before he arrived. She didn't want to leave the girls, but how could she stay? He would surely want her gone. After she had laid bare her feelings. Her feelings for Mister Ellis Dorval, not for the sixth Earl of Beaverbrook. Well, she hadn't really laid bare her feelings, had she? She had run from him. But she should have accepted his offer in that moment, as it was surely much too late now.

She was a mere paid companion. The Earl of Beaverbrook couldn't love one such as she no matter what he might have said in a rare moment in the past.

She was waiting on a reply from Faith Somerton, the young woman Pierce Darby, one of the Northcotts' scholars, had introduced her to. Since she resided at Oxford with her father, she was able to search the library at will to follow any clues they came up with. What had started out as merely one more task she was doing for Lady Evangeline right before the wedding had now become nearly an obsession for Adriana. Once she had finally finagled her way into the search, the scholars had tasked her with keeping track of all the information they managed to accumulate. It kept her busy and involved even as she settled into her new life with the Beaverbrook girls. But it seemed there were far more clues that lead nowhere than any real information. Faith had found the book with the missing page, that had been a thrilling discovery, but hadn't found anything else of import.

And now what was to become of them all?

The treasure hadn't yet been found. Adriana was still in the employ of the Earl of Beaverbrook. And the earl was new. Did that make a difference in her employment? They had signed a contract, something Lady Evangeline had insisted upon. But Adriana didn't think it had specified which earl was entering the contract. So, in essence, she was in Ellis' employ.

He had once professed to "warm feelings" for her. Mere weeks ago. She could hardly credit the short passage of time since it felt as though the world had turned upside down in the meantime. She hadn't denied that she too had such feelings. She would have described her own as hot rather than warm, but that was merely a matter of adjectives. Surely he couldn't still have them. And now he was her employer, so she couldn't have them either.

Chapter Twenty-Four

"How are they holding up?" he asked her in a quiet voice as he met her coming out of the middle girls' bedroom.

Her sigh said it all and revealed her feelings more than he had ever witnessed from her before. Or rather, it was the second most emotions he had ever seen her display. Once before he had heard her express strong emotions very briefly. That memory kept him warm whenever he thought on it.

"As well as can be expected, considering they just buried their father this afternoon."

"So they're much more upset than they have been?" Ellis asked with a frown, watching as she shook her head with a slight smile.

"I wish," she finally admitted. "But no, they still don't seem overly put out by the loss. They seem thrilled that you've taken up residence. Only Cordelia seems to realize this might make things all the more precarious for them."

"Whatever do you mean?"

When she only shook her head, as though she didn't want to tell him, he asked her to accompany him to the library. "We can't properly speak in whispers here in the hallway."

"Is that really appropriate, though, my lord?" she asked, keeping her face averted.

"Of course. I swear I shan't put you to the blush. We have to discuss this. The girls are my responsibility more than ever now. I need to know how they fare."

"Very well." She capitulated easier than he would have expected and quickly led the way to his library where the servants had laid a bright fire.

She began to pace, once more proving how much she had changed from the self-contained young woman he had met in Town months ago. But as though his thought had projected toward her, she caught herself up short and stopped the telling motion, taking a seat in one of the chairs set before the fire.

"Cordelia is upset she won't be able to make her debut in the next Season due to the proper mourning period. She expects you will need to take up her father's quest for a son but your countess won't want her and her sisters in residence. She considers her marriage to be the perfect solution for her sisters."

"I feared as much," Ellis said, running a hand through his hair and wishing he could take up her pacing. "Have my reassurances that this is their home meant nothing?"

"I think it has for the others, but Cordelia has always been the one to feel responsible for everyone. I can't get through to her. She is coming up with the wildest options you could imagine. She's going to make herself ill."

"Should I have a doctor call on her?"

"I'm not sure if it will do any good. Do any of your friends study matters of the heart? I fear it is actually a replacement for grief in her case. She is the only one who really remembers her father before he became so obsessed with having a son. I truly believe the others are unaffected by their loss. They haven't really lost anything. Or rather, their losses are old ones or happened before they were even born. It seems to me that Cordelia must have always held out hope that if her father finally had the boy he was wishing for, then maybe he would once again take an interest in his other children." She paused, taking a deep breath and looking at him as though she didn't want to tell him the rest of her thoughts.

"Tell me, Dria, what is your concern?"

"I'm afraid she is going to blame you, somehow."

"Blame me? How could she possibly do so?" Ellis was taken aback at the very thought.

"You've taken his place so easily. The younger girls are thrilled that you're here. But Cordelia has all these worries and conflicting feelings. I wonder if I ought to take her to Town for the Season anyway. I know she ought to wait at least six months but under the circumstances, do you think anyone would really judge her?"

"Some might, and she really needn't feel pressured. This will always be her home. Do you even think she's ready to go to Town?"

The sound of her gentle sigh caused his gut to tighten. It took everything within his power not to reach for her and gather her into his arms. But he doubted she would welcome such a gesture from him. She had already rejected his pursuit once.

But circumstances were very different now.

That thought almost caused him to swallow his tongue. Could he propose to her again? Should he? He too was in mourning, at least formally so. Would she accept? The sound of rushing wind filled his ears and he wanted to shake his head to clear it but didn't want her to think he was rejecting her words as she had begun to speak once more. He tried to return his attention to the subject at hand.

"I cannot say if she's ready. I feel as though I have gotten to know all the girls quite well in the past several months that we've been together. For me, the time has flown. The days have been so full of activity and conversation. Even though I'm only officially companion to Cordelia and Seraphina, I have found myself spending time with all the girls, even little Primrose, who is such a delight. So am I deluding myself in thinking I know her well? I think she's ready. She thinks she's ready. But I fear she merely *wants* to be ready. That she feels it's her obligation to care for her sisters and this is the only way to do so."

Adriana sighed a little more heavily and looked at him with an imploring expression spread across her lovely features. "Really, it is only the Earl of Beaverbrook who could reassure her that she needn't take such a risk. If she is viewed as unfeeling by the *ton*, she could be rejected outright and have no chance to make a match. Then where would she be in the very reason for her doing so?"

"How can I be of assistance?" Ellis asked immediately. "I will do whatever you think is best."

"Swear to her on whatever she will accept that you will ensure the safety and comfort of her sisters. That they can make their home here or perhaps at Severn, for all the days they are blessed with life. That none of them must wed if they don't so wish."

"Of course," Ellis said when it became evident she had become too embroiled with her own feelings to continue speaking. "Surely they know that already, though, don't they? I mean, I have already said as much to them."

"They need to hear it again, I'm afraid. Most likely on more than one occasion. Think of the life they have led with their father so determined to sire a son. They expect you to pursue the same obsession. And considering how their father's second and third countesses took no interest in them, they cannot expect your countess to do so for mere cousins. In fact, it is to be expected that your countess would wish them to perdition as she cannot be expected to consider them anything but a mere connection, and burdensome ones at that."

"I have no need of a countess any time soon. I am just barely nine and twenty. Surely I have time to start my own nursery. And I've sworn to them to care for them. Even before I inherited, I assured them of my continued care."

"As Severn. It is different now, don't you think?"

"I can see why they might think so. You have raised some interesting points." Ellis cleared his throat from the lump of emotion that was threatening to choke him. "I know of a perfect solution. It would solve all the problems we can currently foresee."

"Truly, my lord?" she asked, her bright, intelligent gaze boring into him with avid interest.

"*You* could become my countess," he said simply, awaiting her response.

He didn't have to wait long. With a gasp she gained her feet and stepped away from him.

"Do not toy with me, my lord. I won't have it."

"But I'm not toying with you, my dearest. Did we not just mere weeks ago tell each other we had developed warm feelings for the other? At the very least, I told you of my feelings. What could be simpler?"

"Whatever might have been said between us, we also concluded that it was completely inappropriate considering our varying stations and my position as your cousins' companion. That has not changed. In fact, our stations have diverged even more drastically than when you were Viscount. Now you are Beaverbrook. I am still barely respectable. You cannot wed the likes of me."

"*We* didn't conclude that, Miss Adams. Only you did. I can do whatever I'd like. As you say, I am the Earl of Beaverbrook." He didn't mean to sound so stuffy, but her rejection stung even more sharply now than the first time. "But you needn't hide behind your lack of nobility. If you have no wish to wed with me that's all you have to say."

Chapter Twenty-Five

Adriana wanted to die. That was the most melodramatic thought she had ever allowed to enter into her mind or heart, but in that moment she felt the hideous sensation all the way down to her toes. It was as though she had ripped out her own heart when she refused his offer. But she couldn't allow him to know that. She didn't need his charity.

And it wasn't that she didn't wish to marry him. She just didn't want it to be for reasons other than personal ones. She truly loved the seven sisters. But they weren't her family. She had obligations toward her own family. That had ruled most of her life. She didn't have any need or desire to take on more of the same thing.

She was so close to finding the treasure with the help of the scholars and the women she had been corresponding with at Oxford, she was certain of it, even if the clues weren't yet proving conclusive. If she could manage to figure it all out, then she would be free and clear from all her obligations. Perhaps she would even stay with the sisters. If the Earl of Beaverbrook would allow that after she had rejected his advances on more than one occasion.

"It isn't that I don't wish to wed, my lord," she began in a tone that even she could hear was nothing but stiffness. "But I don't think marrying for your cousins' convenience is the best foundation upon which to base my future. I am already nearly overcome with obligations to other family members. It might be far too much for me to take on."

When all he did was stare at her with all emotion wiped from his face, Adriana wasn't sure if she ought to continue explaining or run from the room in a panic. She refused to give in to negative emotions, so she stood her ground.

"If we can find Lady Evangeline's treasure, I will be able to free myself of all obligations. I think we're getting close. Some women at Oxford have been helping with the research. Faith found the book the first clue is from. We will surely have it soon. Once I have a piece of that the treasure, whatever it might be, there will never be a need for me to be someone's charitable obligation ever again."

"Charity?" Ellis scoffed, making unease unfurl in her belly. "You think I make you an offer based upon charity? I know you have committed to providing for your family. I think it's rather obscene for them to still be expecting you to support them after all this time, but I understand your sense of obligation, and I would happily assist you with that, with or without your treasure found. Did I not tell you of my great success in business?"

"But don't you see? With your great success, all the less do you need a nobody like me. You could wed with anyone when your mourning is over."

Rather than make her ever more despondent, the sigh he suddenly heaved actually led her to a shaft of optimism.

"I don't want just anyone, Adriana," he said in a low, serious tone. "Don't you recall, mere weeks ago? I thought I had been quite explicit in expressing my feelings toward you. They were not lukewarm or tepid. I love you, Adriana. The woman you are. Not your circumstances. Not your position. Not your obligations or lack thereof. Not even if you found the treasure. I have enough treasure for the lot of us, my cousins included, between Beaverbrook's large coffers and the sales from my extraction process."

Adriana could only stare in disbelief. She couldn't allow herself to accept his words at their face value. What if he changed his mind? Surely, he couldn't know her well enough to make such a declaration. She was nothing special after all. Finally, she had to tell him as much.

"You must be blinded by your obligations to the girls, my lord. I will remain and help you with them, I assure you. You needn't make commitments you will later regret. They have come to mean a great deal to me, as well. I shan't leave them without making sure they are well established beforehand."

Ellis laughed, causing disappointment to flood through her. "I love my cousins, but it is nothing compared to my feelings for you. And I have no intention to wed for their convenience. I merely mentioned them with the hopes that it might sway you in my favour."

A swirl of madness seemed to take up residence in Adriana's mind. Taking a deep breath, she sank back down onto the chair she had recently vacated. "Perhaps you ought to explain," she said in a weak, trembling voice.

Before she could blink, Ellis was on his knees beside her chair, taking possession of her hands that were flailing about like nervous rabbits.

"Miss Adriana Adams, you have quite stolen my heart. For what has felt like an age, I have fought to concede with your decree that it was inappropriate for me to have such feelings for my cousins' companion. But I couldn't quite agree with you. It is merely your occupation. How does that really set you out of bounds? I know I accepted your words the last time we spoke on the matter, but I cannot agree with you. You see, I love you quite madly. Do say you'll accept me. I know you don't wish to be tied down to obligations and being a countess will be terribly inconvenient. But considering how much wealth I seem to possess, I can promise to take you wherever you might wish to go whenever you have the wish to do so if you need a break from it all. You still haven't taken that holiday you spoke of."

When she only stared at him, he started to nervously enumerate all his arguments in an attempt to convince her.

"I shan't inconvenience you overly with childbearing. We don't need to have any children if you truly don't wish it. I'm fairly certain my brother could be convinced to give us his eldest son to be Viscount Severn. I will swear to be nothing like my uncle. If we were to have children, I would be delighted with daughters and will promise not to make you try over and over. I couldn't bear it if you were to die like my aunts. It might be better if we were to satisfy ourselves with my cousins at any rate. And nieces and nephews too. And we could bring your family to live with us if that would be your desire. Just I pray you, do consider it before you reject me once more."

"But why?" she asked simply, praying the tears she wished to indulge in could be kept at bay.

"Why what?"

"Why would you wish to wed with me? I have nothing to offer you."

Ellis's clutch on her hands tightened almost painfully but she basked in their grip.

"Nothing to offer me?" he repeated in an incredulous tone. "You have everything to offer me. I love your wit and your intelligence. Your inquisitive mind. Your patience with these seven rascally females and their numb scull cousin. Your dedication to your own family who don't deserve a whit of it. I love that you are trying to convince me not to love you, but I must tell you that you have failed quite miserably at that."

He would have continued but with a quiet whoop of joy Adriana launched herself into his arms, toppling him back onto his rear where he held her tightly to his chest.

"Is that a maybe, then?" he asked with a chuckle.

The tears she had tried to stave off couldn't be prevented any longer but she joined her own watery chuckle with his.

"That is an emphatic yes if you still mean it. But now what? Will it be perfectly scandalous for us to remain here together until we can marry? What about your mourning?"

"I shall leave in the morning to collect a special license. We could be wed by the end of the week if you'll forgive my eagerness."

Adriana laughed with pure joy while she allowed him to persuade her with his warm kisses for a brief moment. Or perhaps a long moment. Time was of no matter in circumstances such as these.

Before the fire died down in the hearth, though, she recalled them to their senses.

"Will the girls mind?"

"They will be delighted."

"You weren't serious about bringing my family here, though, were you?"

Ellis sighed. "I will do it if it would bring you joy," he answered carefully.

"Do you think it ought to?"

He blinked and stared at her. She could tell he was trying to see into her mind.

"No," he finally answered her rather baldly. "They have not treated you well, ever, from what I can tell.

Perhaps in your infancy, I cannot say, but certainly not since you were a little girl, expected to earn an income to support your family. But if you wanted it, I would do it. For you. Not for them."

"Perhaps we could visit them. And figure out how to extricate me from the obligation."

"That will give me great pleasure," he answered in a very sincere tone.

"Do you want a big wedding like Miss Bastion and her viscount?"

"Nothing would give me a greater fit of the vapours, I can assure you," he said with a laugh.

"Are you absolutely certain? I would be willing."

"But it wouldn't give you the least bit of joy, would it?"

"The end result would," she answered with a grin.

"If you wouldn't mind, what would make me happiest is getting the special license and marrying here, or even at Severn, or perhaps even at the Aldred place with Roderick and Lucy and the other fellows. But with little fuss and no waiting."

"That would be quite delightful, thank you, Lord Beaverbrook," she answered primly, crowing with delighted laughter when he covered her in kisses for her impertinence.

Some time later, Adriana finally climbed to her feet. "That will be enough of that, my lord," she said with mock severity in her voice. "I cannot lose my respectability just before becoming a countess. The best part will be that Cordelia will finally be escorted by Countess Beaverbrook after all."

Ellis laughed. "That was exactly why I proposed, don't you know?" At her gasp of feigned dismay, he had to disabuse her of her inclination to take exception to his words. It was some time later before they finally parted ways.

“What of the treasure hunt, though?” Dria called to him quietly from where she was climbing the stairs after they’d parted once more.

“You shan’t have need of it, but you’re welcome to carry on with the hunt if it amuses you. I was hoping to have a part as well.”

“Or we could pass it along to the others. One could argue that we’ve found our treasure.” Adriana’s heart and feet were light with joy despite the lateness of the hour. She couldn’t wait to tell the girls. They were to be family after all.

Epilogue

Pierce Darby squinted down at the thick paper Lucy Northcott had just handed around to all the fellows at the table.

"We're all invited," she said with a marked note of delight in her voice.

"To what?" Pierce asked with only half his attention on the matter at hand, having left the rest of it back in the room that had been allotted to him for his work.

"Ellis and Adriana are getting married."

"Lucky dog."

"Poor soul."

"Finally."

Pierce had to laugh over the disparate reactions from his friends, the other scholars around the dining table they all shared most evenings. The collection of gentlemen had changed with Sean Smythe, the mathematician, marrying months ago and then Severn inheriting from his uncle and taking up residence at Beaverbrook. Now the fellow was to wed.

"Did Adriana write to anyone with any news of the treasure?" Lincoln Welby, the botanist called out his question. "She's probably too distracted now if Severn has turned her head."

"Last she wrote to me," Jasper Linford called out, "she said she had some connections in Oxford digging into some old books they had found that might be promising."

"All these people getting involved," Sidney Peters, the cartographer, grumbled. "We're going to have to split the treasure too many ways."

"Seems to me Severn has all the treasure he needs now," Welby added in agreement while Pierce just laughed along with the others as Lucy began to scold.

"We should all be happy for Ellis and Adriana," she declared. "In fact, I think it ought to be a house rule. We are obliged to be happy for our friends when they have good news."

"But who's to say getting caught in the parson's mouse trap is good news?" Jasper called out, making Lucy's face fall slightly.

Roderick held up his hand, bringing silence to the table. "I, for one, have to agree with my wife that it is very good news that Ellis has convinced Adriana to marry him. We all quite liked the both of them and I'm sure you all wish them well." He then stopped and turned to his wife with a chuckle. "You're pretty proud of yourself, though, aren't you?"

Lucy's face lit up and all the gentlemen joined in the laughter.

"It's your blasted list, isn't it Roddie? How many women did you have on it? More important how many of us aren't going to be safe for a while."

"You know full well Lucy means the very best for each and every one of you," Roderick stated in a firm tone.

"Of course we do," Pierce agreed immediately. "Unfortunately, sometimes her idea of what's best and our own might not always coincide." This was followed by another round of laughter. "But never mind that, of course we'll all be glad to support the nuptials, but in the meantime, let's get back to figuring out the clues we've got so far."

The End

Want to read about the next scholar's efforts at finding the treasure and running into relationship woes along the way?

Read:

An Heiress and An Astronomer

When handsome scientists and High Society collide, chemistry is sure to follow...

~~~~

New to the Northcott world?
Want to see where the Scholarly Society started out?

Read about Roderick, his brothers, and their friends in the ***Northcott Kinship*** series.

An introductory novella:

Assisting Lord Richmond

She'll *never* love him. Not again, anyway...
~~~~

Book One:

Intriguing Lord Adelaide

She's a wallflower debutante—and his best friend's sister. But one dance could change everything.

About the Author

Wendy learned to read when she was four years old, listening to her mother read great stories to alleviate her loneliness when her big brother started school. Ever since, she's had her head buried in a book. Wendy loves words - historical plaques, signs, the cereal box - but her first love has always been novels, especially of the historical variety.

About fifteen years ago, Wendy's husband dared her to write a book instead of reading them all the time. While she didn't think she could do it, she gave it a shot. To her shock, it grew into her new passion. It started out as a hobby and has become her full-time career.

Wendy believes firmly that everyone deserves a happily ever after. She creates worlds for her readers to escape the everyday for a little while, leaving them feeling upbeat and refreshed when they come out the other side.

When not reading or writing, Wendy can be found traveling the world with her husband, the best adventure companion. Follow those adventures on Facebook or Instagram or join her newsletter on her website wendymayandrews.com

Wendy writes sweet & swoony historical romance - Regency and American Westerns, as well as Contemporary Women's Fiction. She has also started sharing audiobooks on her YouTube channel here:

https://www.youtube.com/@AuthorWendyMayAndrews

Stay in touch:

Website Facebook Instagram TikTok

Stay in touch with Wendy May Andrews
and all her upcoming publishing news

Sign up for her biweekly newsletter at:
wendymayandrews.com

Other books by Wendy May Andrews

See the entire collection!

Scan the QR code below

Printed by Amazon Italia Logistica S.r.l.
Torrazza Piemonte (TO), Italy

60386399R00143